I0760384

Born of Aether

An Elemental Origins Novel

A.L. Knorr

Edited by
S.D. Petersen

Edited by
Teresa Hull

YOU
WILL
BELIEVE.

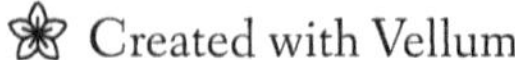
Created with Vellum

Prologue

The moans of the wounded and the dying filled the narrow valley. The full moon, big and bright and already high in the sky, cast its cold blue light over the battle scene. Long thin shadows from arrows and spears embedded in the earth and in flesh slanted across grass, mud, and dark pools of blood. Crows gathered in the branches of nearby trees, their throaty screams alerting other scavengers from miles around. A few brave birds descended to the mud between the bodies, preparing to pick apart their dinner and usher the dead toward the slow transition into dust.

The dark shape of a small black fox darted from the trees to skirt the perimeter of the battlefield. Sniffing the air and stopping to listen, she salivated heavily at the smell of hot blood still pumping from the veins of the dying. At the sound of a moan she bolted into the shadows, her movements quick and sure-footed. She cocked her ears toward the sound, and moved swiftly to investigate.

A dying warrior lay face up to the ghostly moon. Shallow breaths lifted his armored chest with the quiet creak of leather and clink of chainmail. A dark pool gathered between his left arm and his torso as his life poured from his body and soaked into the earth.

The small fox approached on silent paws, stopping to listen before taking a few more steps. Her head low and her ears forward, she inched up to the still-warm and fragrant pool of blood. As a long and final sigh escaped the samurai, her pink tongue darted out to taste the vitamin-rich liquid, the death of one passing on life to another in a cycle as old as the earth itself.

When the fox had raised eight litters, killed and eaten a thousand rodents, escaped a hundred predators, and seen the snows go and the rains come a dozen times, her weak and aged body crawled into a familiar hollow under a juniper for the last time.

The flesh and bone of the samurai whose blood sustained her all those years ago had long since returned to the earth. The memory of that battlefield faded from her fox mind, a nearly insignificant event in her short life. There was room only for the present moment, for the death stealing into her bones and making her shiver.

She settled into her hollow, curling her thick tail over her paws and in front of her nose. She watched the light of another full moon through the thick needles of the bush as her breathing grew shallow and short. She knew what was coming, and she faced it alone, unafraid, and without self-pity. She was tired. She let out a long sigh and her ribs sank as she surrendered.

On any normal day with any normal fox, those ribs would not rise again. But life gives way to life, and as the earthly fox dies, the spirit of the samurai warrior awakens, and the ribs do rise again.

Chapter One

Is there a limit to how many lies one person can tell? My life was so saturated with them that I was afraid to open my mouth for fear of ensnaring myself in one of Grandfather's falsehoods. They say that if you tell a lie for long enough, you'll eventually come to believe it. But that would never happen to me. It couldn't. I would never forget who I was, where I came from, and what had happened to me. It didn't matter how many lies Grandfather commanded me to tell, or what ridiculous story he had dripping from my lips to protect himself. I would always know the truth, and he couldn't change that.

The truth.

The truth was not that I was his granddaughter. I was his captive.

The truth was not that my family died in a plague that swept our village. I had been taken from my home against my will.

The truth was not that my mother was Japanese and my father was Canadian. Both of my parents were Japanese. Grandfather made up the lie to fabricate some connection to this land, to explain our presence in this country.

The truth was not that I was a sixteen-year-old girl. I was nearly a century old.

The truth was not that I was human. I just looked like it.

I disliked walking home alone after school because these were the thoughts that most often clutched my mind. Normally, I walked home with Saxony every day, since we lived in the same neighborhood. But today she had a phone interview with the au pair agency she had applied with, so after saying goodbye to Targa and Georjayna, I had left Saltford High on my own.

Though it was April, the weather was bitterly cold and gray. Snow and ice crusted the streets and bare branches reached up to condemn the cloudy sky.

The suburb we lived in was quiet today. Very few cars passed me, and no one walked the sidewalks. It was too miserable outside for playing, and the playground I passed was abandoned.

Our bungalow was the second to last house on our street. Even from a distance it looked unwelcome. The windows were dark and the curtains drawn. I walked up our front yard, stepped up onto our small deck, and entered our coatroom.

"I'm home," I called out in Japanese as I kicked off my boots. I pulled on my slippers and hung my parka on its hook.

"Akiko," came Grandfather's voice from the small front room.

I poked my head around the corner. "I'm here," I repeated. "Need anything?"

"Sit," Grandfather said, gesturing to the couch across from his chair. His laptop was open and it sent a blue glow onto his lined face.

I frowned. When Grandfather asked me to sit, it usually meant he had something more complicated for me to do. He hadn't asked me to sit in years. Most of my commands these days were mere errands—groceries, translating something for him, mailing something at the post office, making dinner, doing laundry, cleaning the house, shoveling the front walk. I was the world's most exotic house keeper.

I sat and waited.

He steepled his withered hands and gazed at me from across the coffee table. "My name is Daichi Hotaka," he said.

My mouth dropped open. I could do nothing but stare. My heart began to pound. Something was going to change, something had happened. My mind raced. What had happened? Why, after all this time, was he finally telling me his name? My hands instantly felt ice-cold. I didn't know what to say, so all I did was wait, skin prickling with anticipation. With effort, I closed my mouth.

"I have been searching for something that was stolen from me many years ago." Nothing about his countenance changed, but I could sense a vibration of excitement about him that I had never felt before. "I have finally found it."

He reached a hand out and spun the laptop to face me.

My eyes dropped to the screen. It showed a video on YouTube entitled 'Ryozen Museum to Display Artifacts from the Bakamatsu Period. Early summer.' My eyes scanned the text below the video: *The Ryozen Museum of History in Kyoto, Japan, specializes in the history of the Bakumatsu period and the Meiji Restoration. The museum is dedicated to the often violent events that brought an end to the Tokugawa regime at the climax of the Edo Period.*

Daichi had frozen the screen on a closeup of a wooden rack carrying four samurai short swords. Three of them were in black sheaths, and one of them was in a blue sheath with some kind of pattern on it. He pointed a twisted finger at the short sword with the blue sheath. It looked like the design on the sheath might be of trees, but the screen was blurry so it was difficult to make out.

"Bring me this wakizashi," he said.

My eyes widened and flew to his face. Had I heard him correctly? I swallowed hard, my mind a torrent of questions. This was more than just an errand. This was a mission, and probably an illegal one. "It is in Kyoto, Grandfather," I said. "You want me to go back to Japan?" A torrent of emotions crashed through me like a tsunami. After all this time, he was going to let me visit our homeland? Alone? We hadn't been back in Japan since we left over a lifetime ago – me caged and in the form of a bird. Grandfather had never expressed a desire to go back, but then again, he rarely expressed desires more complex than hunger. I had long ago given up hope of setting foot in Japan again.

He nodded. "It will be on display soon, and not for very long." He placed his hands flat on his thighs and leaned forward. "The time for this is now. I have spent years looking for this sword. We may never have another chance."

"I am to—" I paused, processing his command and what it meant. "Steal it?"

His eyes gleamed and he stared at me unblinking. He took a long slow breath and each moment that passed raised gooseflesh on my skin. "You bring me this wakizashi, and I will give you your freedom."

My head was still spinning a few days later. I sat through my classes in a daze, and avoided spending too much time with Saxony since even she was bound to notice my distraction. Every night I lay awake praying that Daichi wasn't playing some kind of sick joke on me, that he wouldn't retract his offer. I had chosen to walk home alone every day so I could think. If I kept this up, Saxony was going to chase me down.

I scuffed my feet along the sidewalk, kicking chips of ice skittering down the pavement. This had to be my last solitary stroll home, and thankfully the shock had worn off enough that I thought I could hang out with my friends without alerting them that something big was happening.

Daichi barked at me from the kitchen as soon as I stepped into the house. "Akiko?"

"Here," I called, taking off my jacket and boots. My heart leapt into my throat and I fought to wrestle my irrational dread back into its place. Just because he had something to say didn't mean he was going to withdraw the offer. I took a breath, put my hat and mitts into the wooden bin under the coatrack, and pulled on my slippers. I padded down the hall to the kitchen and immediately began to warm up. Daichi kept the heat cranked up no matter the season.

He sat at the kitchen table staring out into our snow-covered back yard. A small cardboard box sat on the table in front of him. He looked at me as I entered.

"Sit."

I sat, heart pounding in my ears, and pleading inside that he wasn't about to rescind his offer.

He pushed the cardboard box across the table toward me. "You will need this."

I stifled an audible sigh of relief. He was furnishing me with some kind of necessity, not calling the whole thing off. I slid the box closer and opened it. Unfolding the tissue paper revealed black fabric. Bemused, I pulled out the fabric and held it out. It was so soft and thin that it slipped through my fingers like air. Dangling it by the top, I could finally see what it was. It had short sleeves and the body of it was so short I doubted that it would even come to my knees.

"A bathrobe, Grandfather?" On Georjayna, it wouldn't even cover her butt. "Uh... thank you."

I spotted a small bulge in the pocket on the front of the robe. I fished out a pair of thin slippers in the same material. As footwear, they would fall apart within days. I couldn't help my look of confusion.

"They are one hundred percent silk," Daichi said matter-of-factly.

"Oh?"

He took the robe from me and got to his feet stiffly. He brushed the cardboard box to the side and lay the robe out flat on the table. He spread the arms out in a perfect 'T', tucked the slippers into the front pocket and began to roll the robe from the bottom up. Folding it over and over into a stripe of fabric no thicker than an inch, he picked the length of it up and looped it around my neck twice, snug enough that if he'd pulled it any tighter I might have coughed. He tied the ends in a knot and stepped back.

I looked up at him, fingering the odd scarf. Was the old man finally losing his mind? I swallowed and felt the silk tighten.

"Grandfather," I began. "I'm confused."

"Become a bird," he said.

When he gave me an order, I could no more hold back the tide than I could prevent myself from executing it. I phased into a small gray chicken, my clothing falling past my small feathered body to the floor. I landed on the edge of my chair and almost slipped off the smooth wooden seat. I squawked and flapped, my claws scrabbling for purchase. The silk loosened from around my neck but it stayed draped around my chicken shoulders.

"Become a bird that can fly," Daichi barked with exasperation.

I phased into a crow and hopped up on the table, tilting my head at Daichi. The silk robe hung from my neck like an absurd scarf, but I could barely feel its weight.

Daichi opened our back door and a burst of cold air swept the kitchen. "Fly to the ocean and return," he commanded. "Do not lose the silk!"

I hopped to the edge of the table, hooked my claws over the rim, and took off through the open door. I dropped low toward the ground, picked up a gust of wind and swooped upward. Up and up I spiraled, the silk hanging from my neck in front of my wings. I didn't feel the cold nearly as much when I was a bird, and the wind increased as I approached the ocean. I swept out over the beach, cawing my pleasure hoarsely at this brief freedom. I circled over the waves and headed back to the house. Well-kept yards covered in snow swept by beneath me as I passed over our suburb.

The back door to our kitchen opened and I slowed down and flew inside.

"Go to your room and become human," came the next order.

I whooshed past Daichi, landed in the hall, and hopped into my bedroom. I beaked the door closed and phased back into my human form. I stood there naked in front of the full-length mirror, my chest rising and falling as I caught my breath. The silk robe was once again tight around my throat.

Daichi had put my clothes on my bed. I pulled them on and went back to the kitchen where he was once again seated at the table, waiting.

His eyes, deep in their wrinkled folds, dropped to the black silk around my neck. "It stayed," he said.

"Yes."

"Still confused?" he asked, folding his gnarled fingers on the table and leaning forward.

"A little." I sat down across from him. "I understand you want me to have clothing for when I arrive in Japan, but—"

"It will not disappear," he said, cutting me off. "It will not disappear in the Æther."

I frowned. I wanted to ask him how he could know that for sure, but I knew what the answer would be. The same it always was, the non-answer.

Daichi leaned forward and patted the back of my hand in a rare moment of contact. He gave me the non-answer anyway. "I was old before I met you," he said. He got up and walked in his slow plodding way toward the living room where he would wait until our evening meal was ready.

"What do you want for dinner, Grandfather?" I asked. "Besides rice."

He paused and looked back. Amusement was just a ghost at his lips, but the upward twitch of his mouth was unmistakable. "Chicken." He disappeared around the corner.

I smiled and untied the knot of silk at my throat. Funny how after so many years together, even under unhappy circumstances, there could still be some kind of humor between us.

Chapter Two

Saxony closed her locker and pulled her hood up over her wild curls. She hooked her arm through mine. "Come on, I'll walk you home. It's been too long." She eyed the gloomy sky outside. "Why did I put away my winter stuff? It was so nice last week."

"You always put it away too early," I said, smiling. Every year was the same. "We live near the Atlantic—don't you know by now that spring means snow and freezing rain?"

"Don't swear," she said. She pulled a folded yellow document from her pocket. "Look what I got today." She waved it in front of my face.

"A subpoena?"

"Noooooooooo." She drew out the word with artificial annoyance.

"A parking ticket?"

"No. Stop that."

I gave a fake and exaggerated gasp. "Jury duty?"

Her eyes grew wide and she gasped, too. "How did you know?"

"What?" I gaped at her.

She whacked my shoulder. "No. Shut up and listen, would you?"

"A love letter?" I tried one more time.

"Yes!" She bounced up and down. "From the au pair agency in Toronto. They have a place for me in Venice. Guess who is spending the summer in bella Italia?"

"No way." I held the school's front door open for her and we walked out into a fine wet mist.

"Way. And I can't get there soon enough," she said, pulling her collar up around her ears. "No one should live here. Brrrrrrrrr." She shivered. "Would you come visit me there?"

"Uh..." The idea of visiting Saxony in Italy during the summer was heavenly. "Grandfather—"

"I know, I know," she interrupted. "He'll never let you go to Europe. I was completely shocked when he let you sleep over at Georjie's house last year for her birthday. It's the only nice thing he's done for you like, ever. Have I ever told you that I'm not all that fond of your grandfather?"

I smiled and hooked her elbow as we took the concrete steps down to the sidewalk. "A couple of times. Even though you've never met him."

"A," she said, holding up a long finger, "whose fault is that?" She held up a second finger. "And two, I dislike him on principle. He never lets you do anything fun. It's like he's got you on an invisible leash."

I had to smile at her description. It was worse than a leash. I wondered what she'd say if I told her he wasn't my grandfather and that he'd basically stolen my soul. I cleared my throat. I was bound not to say any such thing. Instead, I said, "You might be surprised to learn that he's sending me to Japan."

"He's never once even let you have me over, your best friend—" Saxony continued, but then froze abruptly and pulled me to a stop. "Wait. What?"

Her face had gone even paler than normal, quite an accomplishment for a redhead with a porcelain complexion.

"Not for good," I said quickly. "Just for the summer."

"Really? I stand corrected. What for?"

I gave Saxony the lie that Daichi had told me to say. "He wants me to spend the summer with the Japanese side of my family, since I never knew them. They live in a small village in the mountains on the east side. It's supposed to be beautiful."

Saxony narrowed her eyes and studied my face.

"What?" I tugged on her arm to get her walking again.

"I'm just trying to figure out if you're happy about it." She matched me stride for stride. She gripped my elbow, and didn't take her eyes from my face.

My heart sped up the way it always did when I was under scrutiny, even from those I trusted. Too many lies had passed my lips for me to ever feel completely comfortable with anyone digging for more information. The irony of the situation was that I was dying to tell my story to my friends. What a relief it would be to express the suffering and loss I'd endured. I had been alone in it for so long. I shot Saxony a side eye. "And?"

She studied me intensely.

"Are you okay?" I asked. "You're not blinking."

She gave a sigh. "I gave up trying to read you about a week after meeting you." She relaxed her grip on my elbow. "So, *are* you happy about it? Do you even want to go?"

I shrugged and tried to put a neutral expression on my face. I had become a master at hiding my emotions—from my captor and from my friends. One of the reasons I liked spending time with Saxony was that she usually didn't dig too hard and she talked a lot. She was the extrovert I was safe hiding behind. But as she'd gotten older, she'd gotten better at asking questions.

"It is what it is," I answered.

She groaned. "I hate when you say that. Fine, have it your way." She stepped around a patch of ice and pulled her collar up to her chin again. "Did I tell you that Jack plastic-wrapped the toilet last night? Was *I* that brain-damaged at fifteen?"

As Saxony talked, I relaxed into her world. Her family was so normal, so loving. Hers was a life I could watch from the outside with envy. Georjayna struggled with a mom who didn't care enough, and Targa struggled with a mom she felt responsible for. Only Saxony had the stability of an intact family. I wondered if it was where she got her confidence from. I'd seen her walk into a party where she knew no one and within an hour she knew everyone's name, had endeared some of the girls to herself, and had most of the guys following her around like puppies. She also annoyed some people to no end because she was always talking, laughing, always the center of attention. She was the perfect companion to divert eyes away from me. Saxony, Georjie, and Targa were my first close human friends. They'd become my anchor and the only good thing I had in my captivity. My mind went back to Daichi's words.

Bring me this wakizashi, and I'll give you your freedom.

Freedom.

I had been staring down the barrel of an endless, useless life. Servant to the whims of an elderly Japanese man who should have been dead a hundred years ago and who never shared his motivations with me for any choice he made. Who never told me why he'd brought me here, what he wanted, or how I might move on with my life one day.

Until now.

There was no way Daichi could be happy with our life the way it had become. I had never actually seen him happy. Why anyone as miserable as Daichi would even want to be immortal was beyond me. The waste of it sickened me. It twisted in my stomach and made me want to scream.

Every night for decades, Daichi had me phase into a bird and locked me in a cage. All I wanted at that time was to remain human, to have human dreams again, and sleep in a soft warm bed. Then when he finally let me remain human and had a bed delivered to the house for my room, the nightmares started. He never said anything about my night terrors. He never forced me to go back to my cage. I did that all on my own. The passing of time was easier to bear in bird-form, and I didn't have nightmares. It was a little better now. Sometimes I spent the night in my cage, sometimes in my bed, depending on my mood.

When he enrolled me in school and forced me to spend hours studying English and practicing to eliminate my Japanese accent, it served two purposes. It equipped me to be his go-between in the foreign place he'd moved us to, and it kept me so busy that I fell into bed exhausted and dreamed about grammar instead of that fateful day in the woods when my sister had betrayed and abandoned me.

When I finished the high school on the south side of Saltford, he moved me to a school in the north and started me over again. I was more than three years into my cycle at Saltford High and this time around it was impossible not to ace every class. I had no trace of a Japanese accent left, and the North American way of life had become my way of life. I couldn't allow myself to dream of what I would do if I had my life back. I wondered if Daichi felt even a hint of guilt about keeping a creature as powerful as I was behind bars for his own selfish purpose...whatever that was. A surge of dragonflies spiraled up from my stomach and battered my ribs from the inside when I thought about what little seemed to remain between me and my freedom.

"Hey?" Saxony squeezed my arm.

"What? Sorry." I blinked. We were in front of my house already.

"I said, when do you leave?"

"We haven't booked my ticket yet, but it'll be shortly after the school year ends."

Saxony nodded. "Same time as me. Let's make sure we get the four of us together before you and I go."

"Sure, that would be great."

We said goodbye and I wandered up the cinderblock steps to our bungalow. A shiver of anticipation went through me as I thought about my impending flight. I would be flying, but there was no need to book a plane ticket. I'd be making this journey on my own wings, the wings of one of the few birds that could fly high enough to reach the Æther. Thirty thousand feet up, somewhere in the vicinity of earth's ozone layer, lay the home of all spiritual energy and the force that had made my sister and I each what we were.

Chapter Three

"They're in the back yard," Liz said, holding the front door open for Saxony and me. Her Prada bifocals were perched on the end of her nose. Her blond hair was still perfectly coiffed, even at the end of a long day, but the dark smudges beneath her eyes gave away her exhaustion. Georjayna's mom had made partner at her law firm a few years back. Since then, I hadn't seen her without the dark circles. And since then, Georjie had felt almost motherless. "Come on through. It's the warmest evening we've had so far," Liz said. "But it's still cool. There are blankets at the fire pit for you."

"Thanks, Liz," Saxony said as we stepped into the massive marble entrance way. Four large panels of mirrored sliding doors hid their coat closet, and a wide curved staircase led downstairs to their indoor pool and games room where I had first met Saxony and Georjayna. A matching set curved upward to their loft and library.

“You know how to get there,” Georjie's mother replied, shutting the door behind us. "Have fun." She gave us a stiff smile and disappeared down the hall toward her office.

I followed Saxony past the enormous kitchen and through the sliding doors into Georjie's backyard. A few stars were visible in the cloak of darkness over Saltford, and a gentle breeze kissed my skin as we crossed the deck. Georjayna's house was built on a bluff overlooking the ocean and the lights of our small city peppered our view. The ocean stretched out black and endless into the dimming horizon.

"Hey!" Targa called from her place by the fire, stretching her arms wide. She had a bag of marshmallows in one hand. "You're here!"

"Yeah well, we heard there were s'mores here," said Saxony as we crossed the grass.

The fire crackled merrily, sending sparks toward the darkening sky. Targa and Georjayna's faces were lit by the dancing firelight, and they both had blankets draped over their legs. If I wasn't mistaken, there was a kind of excitement in both of them that hadn't been there at school.

"Come grab a seat." Georjie patted the blanket on the Adirondack chair beside her. "Iced tea?"

"Absolutely," I said.

Saxony and I settled into our chairs as Georjayna poured us drinks.

"Targa has news," Georjie said.

"Lemme guess," said Saxony. "You've developed a crush on the new guy they hired at the body shop?" She took her iced tea from Georjayna and poked at the ice cubes with her straw.

"There's a new guy at the body shop?" Georjie asked. "How do you even know these things? *Why* do you know these things?"

"RJ," said Saxony, and took a swallow of her drink. "I was with him when he picked up a part for his car yesterday. Dude is cute. The new guy, not my brother," she clarified.

"Your brother is pretty cute, too," laughed Georjie. Pretty cute didn't do RJ justice, the guy was a dark-haired Adonis.

Saxony rolled her eyes in a *whatever* gesture. "This new guy's got that tortured mechanic thing going on." Saxony reached for two roasting sticks leaning against Georjie's chair and handed one to me.

"Ah, yes" smiled Georjie. "The tortured mechanic. Targa's dream guy."

Targa laughed. "Good guess. But, no," she said, handing the bag of marshmallows to Saxony. "I'm going to Poland."

"That was my next guess," said Saxony sardonically. "You're going *where*?"

"Gdansk," said Targa and Georjie together.

"That's a thing?" Saxony's eyes were wide as platters. She held a marshmallow over her stick, ready for piercing but forgotten in the moment.

"It's a port city in the Gulf of Danzig," I said with a grin, "on the Baltic sea." It was easy to look super smart when you've been through school a few times.

"No surprise you know all about it, Jeopardy." Saxony threw the marshmallow at me. I caught it, pierced it with my own stick and held it out over the flames. "Why are you going there, T?"

"The Bluejackets took on a salvage contract there. It's a private one, for a rich Polish guy. He's setting us up with accommodation and whatever the team needs to do the salvage. My mom told Simon she'd only go if she could take me, so." Targa shrugged and grinned. "We leave in a few days."

"That's amazing, Targa," I smiled across the fire at my friend.

She smiled back and held my gaze. "Thanks, Akiko." Her eyes flicked to Georjayna. "Georjie has some news, too."

"You're going to Ireland after all?" I guessed.

"No way!" said Saxony. "For real, Georjie?"

"For real," Georjie said. "I haven't told Liz yet, but—"

"She'll be thrilled," finished Saxony with another eyeroll. "Finally got the place to herself."

"Easy," said Targa quietly.

"What?" Saxony sat up straighter. "It's true, isn't it?" She turned to Georjie. "Didn't you say that your mom was trying to oust you for the summer?"

"It's one thing for Georjie to say it," I offered. "It's another thing when someone else says it."

"Sorry," Saxony slouched and pressed her lips together.

Georjie sighed. "No, it's fine. Call it what it is, right?"

"And call Ireland green and gorgeous. How bad could it be?" said Targa. "I love the Irish accent."

"Except for Akiko, we'll all be in Europe," Saxony said, bouncing in her seat. "We have to promise to text, okay?"

Georjayna and Targa agreed easily. I frowned. I didn't know what the task of retrieving the wakizashi was going to mean yet. If I committed to text the girls often, and then somehow couldn't, they'd get worried. It would be better if I set the expectation now that I wouldn't be chatty during my mission.

"I'll try," I said. "I'm just not sure how good the signal will be where I'm going. From what I know the family is kind of remote and I'm not sure how fond they are of technology."

"Who doesn't have wifi these days?" asked Georjayna with a look of horror. "Seriously, where is your grandfather sending you, to a mountain cave?"

I smiled to cover the anxiety burbling up in my stomach. "Who knows. His descriptive skills are scanty at best."

"How come your grandfather isn't going with you?" Targa asked. "Doesn't he want to go back home for a visit, too?"

I kept my face neutral. It would be best to get off the subject of my trip to Japan, and Daichi, as soon as possible. "He's too old for that kind of traveling now," I said, and cast my eyes down at the fire to shut down any further questions.

We fell into a companionable silence, but I felt Targa and Georjayna's eyes on me for several minutes. I knew they wanted to dig, but I'd trained them well not to expect answers. Saxony slurped her iced tea and I almost laughed. She was so predictably unsuspicious.

Targa had actually met Daichi once at the farmer's market. It had been a tense moment for me, introducing one of my best friends to my captor. I'd awkwardly introduced him as 'Grandfather' since I hadn't known his real name at that point. When she'd held out her hand for a handshake and he'd just given her a cold stare, I had almost breathed an audible sigh of relief. If he was unfriendly, Targa would be less likely to try and have a relationship with him.

Saxony finally broke the quiet. "Let's promise to have a sleep over when everyone gets back." Her gaze swung to me, the only one who might risk not getting permission to come.

I smiled to myself when I thought that by that time, I wouldn't have to ask Daichi's permission to spend an overnight with my friends. I would be a free woman by then. Everyone agreed, and me along with them.

"How do you know the Æther will drop me out in Japan?" I asked Daichi as I set my backpack down on the kitchen table. "I've never ridden it before."

"I was old before I met you," said Daichi. He had a handful of Japanese yen laid out on the table. He stacked it and inserted it into an envelope. "Memorize this address," he said, pushing a scrap of paper toward me with a handwritten address in Kyoto on it. "And the number below will be the combination to open your storage unit.

Daichi set a piece of white paper out on the table as well as an ink pad. He opened it up and held out his hand. "Give me your thumb," he said.

I let him press my thumb into the ink, and then stamp the paper with my thumbprint.

"Do you need me to scan that for you?" I asked.

He shook his head. "By now, I'm better with technology than you are."

I gave a half-smile as I washed my thumb off at the sink. He was probably right about that. Who would have ever thought it possible that a man born in the 1800s would take to computers so well.

"Have you packed what you need?"

I nodded. "I think so. Two sets of clothes, a pair of sneakers, a small purse with my ID, the bank card you gave me, my passport, and my cell phone and charger." I took one last look in my backpack and frowned. "I'm pretty sure it's illegal to courier a passport and cash, unless you're the government. What if they get stuck in customs?" I shuddered to think of opening the storage unit in Japan, finding it empty, and trying to execute my orders while in possession of only a silk bathrobe and useless slippers.

"It's illegal to steal an artifact from a museum as well," said Daichi, tilting his chin down and giving me a look. "If there is trouble, you find a way to call me."

Emboldened by how Daichi had taken me into his confidence with this task, I suggested an alternative. Something I had never done with any command before this one. "If the wakizashi is that important to you, why don't you just make the museum an offer for it? I can execute the transaction for you." I had no idea how Daichi had kept us financially looked after all these years, but he had to have a lot of cash at his disposal. As far as I was aware, he had never worked since the day he had captured me. Unless he had some online business I was unaware of, which, come to think of it, wasn't hard to believe.

Daichi's face sank into an expression akin to regret. "Once. I could have. But now...it has taken too long just to find it." His expression cleared. "Enough questions. When you have the wakizashi, you call me."

"I will have to fly back on a plane with it," I mused. "There is no way it will stay intact through the Æther, and I definitely couldn't carry it all the way home as a bird. I'd drown in the ocean a few miles off the coast, no matter what species I became."

"Don't worry about that," said Daichi gruffly. "Focus on getting it out of the museum without getting caught. Let me worry about the rest."

My stomach did a flip of terror at the word 'caught' and I swallowed hard. The realization of what I was going to do began to sink in. Somehow, I was supposed to break this artifact out of a museum without setting off any alarms, without alerting any staff, and without any patrons seeing me do it. Would the ability to phase into a bird even be of any use to me in this scenario? I closed my eyes. *It's for your freedom, Akiko.* I had to find a way.

As though he could sense my rising tension, Daichi stood up. "It's time," he said.

"I'm ready." I sounded more confident than I felt. I didn't want to give Daichi any reason to doubt me and retract the opportunity. There was too much at stake for me to fail.

Daichi and I made eye contact and held it for a moment. "Luck, destiny, and the Æther are both on our side," he said. He put a gnarled hand on my upper arm. "Now, go."

"Goodbye, Grandfather," I said. I went to my bedroom and shucked my clothing. I tied the silk robe around my neck and phased into a common crane. Within my slender wings was the ability to soar higher than almost any other species. I hopped down the hall and back into the kitchen.

Daichi stood at the back door, one gnarled hand on the door handle. He opened the door and cool fresh air swirled into the kitchen, beckoning me. I strutted past Daichi's legs and through the now towering exit. The bright afternoon sky stretched out above me, endless space and freedom.

I hopped off the porch as a gust of wind blew through the yard, then I caught the updraft and pointed my beak to the sky. I didn't look back as the house and Daichi spiraled away beneath me, shrinking to the size of monopoly pieces. Thirty-thousand feet up. Into the ozone. That was where I would find it—the Æther. The wind picked up and blew me around, helping me surge ever upward. The air grew cold and wet as I disappeared into thick clouds and could see nothing but bright fog. Up and up and up I continued, my wings tireless and powerful. The silk at my neck became damp with condensation.

The air grew thin and still I flew. Breaking through the clouds, I didn't look down at the tops of the fluffy cotton below me. Up and up I spiraled, resting my wings and soaring on updrafts where I could. The atmosphere above me stretched out like an endless becalmed sea—a desert of silence and space.

The snapping of distant thunder and the flash of a bright light took my breath away. My vision went first. Or was I just so high up that there was nothing to see? Silence closed in around me. Surely, I had to be close. So close. I lost all sense of up or down, left or right. My senses shut down. I felt no wind any longer, no cold. The aching of my wings and the feel of air brushing against my feathers faded away. The sensation of the damp silk robe at my neck disappeared. I felt nothing. Nothing but a small, cold, empty place deep inside me. Like I'd swallowed an ice cube and there it sat, melting in my gullet.

I surrendered to the Æther, to the trust I had that it would carry me where I needed to go. All I had up here was that cold empty space inside me, and my memories.

Chapter Four

There came a point when I realized that my parents treated my sister Aimi and I differently than other parents treated their children. Maybe it was observing the way children were told to keep silent whenever we ventured out in the village. We had chores and responsibilities, but we were allowed to speak and were asked for our opinions. We were permitted to take our creature shapes as we wished as long as we were far from town and we knew for certain we were not being observed.

Aimi would take her Kitsune shape, always a fox, and I would take to my Akuna Hanta wings. I could take the shape of any bird I wanted, though how that meant I could hunt demons I couldn't have explained. We would play in our forest for hours, passing our youth as happy as any child could ever wish to be. As we grew older, our parents would inform us of the goings on in the village, and of changes in Father's business, good or bad. I began to see a pattern in what happened after they did this. If something wasn't working out in our favor, our parents would lay the situation out to Aimi and I over dinner. Aimi would listen intently, and say very little. But a short time afterward, the winds of fortune would shift in our direction and everything would turn out okay.

No one else in our village knew what we were and so never gave us any special treatment. Least of all the neighbor's son, Toshi, who played tricks on me relentlessly. He would snatch the sticks from my hair on a windy day, making the long black strands whip around and become hopelessly tangled. He'd drop a toad in my lap and run away laughing as I gagged with revulsion. He'd wait behind our outhouse until I needed to use it and then throw caterpillars in through the moon shaped window. The path I took into the woods to gather plants and mushrooms for my mother wound by his house and he waited in the bushes to jump out at me and set my heart to pounding.

I came to abhor my daily trek by his house so I took great pains to make a new and secret path to avoid falling into his traps. A game of cat and mouse ensued, where Toshi would wait until he knew I was leaving the house and follow me, trying to discover my secret path. I would lead him through the woods, meander through the swamp, up over the rock slabs, and through the brambles until his father would call for him and he'd have to abandon the chase.

I had begun to feel that I had won when he stalked me less and less. Soon weeks would pass without him hounding me and I began to relax. Then I began to miss his attentions. I learned rapidly as I became a teenager that Toshi was unlike other boys of our village. He did not look down on girls and shun their company. Boys and girls were strictly segregated in different schools and social activities, but that had never prevented Toshi from paying attention to me. He always had a good-natured smile for me, even as he teased me mercilessly, there was no malice in it.

Eventually thoughts of Toshi faded away. Life went on and my duties changed from those of a little girl to those of a young woman. I became wrapped up in the secret world inside our own house. I played only with Aimi, as the other girls in our village were as boring as worms by comparison. She whispered secrets of the Æther to me in the dark of our shared room, and we talked of venturing further abroad in our creature shapes, and even of eavesdropping on the closed-door meetings the men of the village attended, to see who was going to be wedded to whom next. It would have been strictly for the thrill of being there when no one knew it, because our father would come home and tell us anyway.

Several summers had gone by before I gathered my herb basket and decided impulsively to take the old path, the one that wandered by Toshi's house.

The rhythmic sharp sound of chopping wood echoed off the trees and rock slabs. Expecting to find his father, I rounded the bend and their yard came into view. My body became still as my eyes fell on the man wielding the axe, but my mind was a tempest. Broad square hands gripped the wooden handle, and his thick black hair was tied half-back to keep out of his eyes. The high forehead and widow's peak reminded me of drawings I had seen of ancient samurai.

I could not have stopped myself from staring even if I had been in a crowd. Sweat-slick skin pulled taut over the figure of a grown man. He moved with the grace of someone at home inside himself, not the gangly clumsiness of the boy I remembered. How could this creature be Toshi? Could he have changed this much? What had happened to the boy who used to torture me?

A twig snapped under my foot and he looked up. His eyes fell on me and we gazed at one another. There he was. Toshi. He squinted toward me, the sun in his eyes. It took a moment, but recognition melted the line between his brows and an enormous grin split across his face. He lifted a sweat-drenched arm, seemingly unembarrassed to be caught naked to the waist.

"Akiko!" he called, a little out of breath.

I gasped as he dropped his axe and crossed the back yard with an easy stride, his footsteps silent in his fabric boots. He made his way through the trees and into the shade, stopping not far from me.

"I can see you more easily now," he said. "I almost didn't recognize you. When did you become a woman?"

"When did you become a man?" I countered, unable to stop the spread of my own grin. I knew that no other girls in our village would dare address a boy in this way. The respect my father gave to Aimi and me in the privacy of our home gave me confidence unheard of in other girls.

Toshi inhaled at my daring, and was perhaps emboldened by it. His teak-colored eyes took me in, the only part of this man who reminded me of the boy I once knew. "But you're beautiful!"

I laughed with delight. It seemed Toshi also did not like the formality normally imposed upon young people of our age. Men did not speak to women like this. I was already surprised he'd approached me, as it was custom for young men and women to have a chaperone in order to be together. Apparently, Toshi didn't care.

"And you are bold," was all I could think to say, as heat flushed my cheeks.

He laughed and it too, reminded me of the boy. "We are old friends."

"Friends? You tortured me to no end when we were young. That was friendship?" I raised my eyebrows and crossed my arms, my basket dangling over my forearm. "I hope we never become enemies."

He dropped his gaze and chuckled, a black strand of hair falling over his face. "Don't you know," he said as his eyes flicked back up to mine, "that's what boys do when they like a girl?"

I gasped. My whole body flushed with an unexpected heat. Where had little Toshi gotten his confidence from? My heart swelled, and just like that, he had me. His good-natured, lop-sided grin swept my feet out from under me and I knew what I wanted then. More than any Hanta life, I wanted Toshi.

"And men?" I asked, breathless. "What do men do when they like a woman?"

His eyes widened in surprise. "I see I am not the only one who has found courage."

He took a step forward and I took a step back, both of us smiling. My heart pounded like a hammer and everything in me had come alive in a way that it never had before. I never knew these feelings were possible.

"Men go after what they want," he said, taking a lunge toward me.

I squealed and ran, lifting my skirts as I bolted away from him. My basket discarded and forgotten, I tore through the woods, fueling my legs with Hanta fire. Laughing, we pelted through the trees, Toshi hot on my heels. His fingertips would graze my shoulder, my waist, but always I would dodge away. His surprise at my speed delighted me even further. What amazed me even more, I realized—as the trees whizzed by and I scrambled up over the rock slabs and boulders—was that I trusted him completely. The only other man in whose company I felt safe and respected up to that point was my father. Why that was, I could not explain, it was only something I could feel and settle into.

My heart in my throat and Toshi's footfalls behind me, I ascended the boulders leading to the rock slab overlooking the coast and Tai Island. It was my favorite place in the world. It might have been more popular, except it was so difficult to get to. By the time I crested the last boulder, my legs were shaking, my body was as hot as a coal, and my chest was heaving. Toshi finally caught me and swung me around in the sunlight as it beamed down on the huge clifftop. Moss cushioned our footfalls and tiny stones scattered as we kicked them rolling with our slippered feet. The wind picked up tendrils of our hair and cooled my face and neck.

His face was so close to mine and his grin was all for me. I thought I would burst with the pleasure of the moment. Toshi's chest and shoulders heaved under my hands as he caught his breath, his slick skin sliding under my palms. I had never touched any man this way before, yet somehow, it felt so natural. His hands closed around my waist and he looked down at me.

"Why did you stay away for so long?" he asked.

"Well," I brushed strands of hair back from my face, "you were a thorn in my side." I swallowed and panted, my heart still pounding in the cage of my ribs.

"Akiko," he said and put his forehead to mine. The sun reflected in one of his eyes and lit it from within, as golden as honey. His hands squeezed my waist. "Tell me you knew."

"Knew?" I pulled back and gazed at him, palms on his arms.

"Tell me you knew that I loved you. From the moment I first stood near you and was intoxicated by your scent, by your being. I loved you. I love you still."

My nerves made me laugh, in spite of the seriousness that had taken over his face. "My scent?"

He leaned down and put his face next to mine with a soft inhale. Shivers coursed up my spine as he breathed me in. "Like the air after a thunderstorm. No one else smells this way."

I closed my eyes, letting him hover there. If my mother had seen me she would have been horrified, maybe even ashamed of how wanton Toshi had made me. But I didn't care. I felt alive, and no one would ever see us here. This was my clifftop, mine and Aimi's, and now it belonged to Toshi, too.

"I had no other way to get close to you, other than to harass you," he said quietly, his breath grazing my neck. "It was the only way I could have your smell, your smile."

I laughed and stepped back. "I don't remember smiling at you—cursing you was more like it."

"You did smile," he said, taking my hand as we walked to the edge of the rock slab to overlook the ocean. "You always had a smile for me, even when I was horrible. Tell me I can have that smile for the rest of my life?"

I gasped. "Our parents—"

"Yes, I know. We have to get their approval. It won't be difficult, Akiko. We are a perfect match. And my father has always said there was something special about the Susumu girls. You will see." He pulled me around to face him again. He put his fingers under my chin and lifted my face. "Say yes. I will pledge my life to make you happy, keep you safe, and make sure you want for nothing."

I thought my heart would leap from my chest and into his hands. He was completely irresistible. I could not remember loving him when I was a little girl, but my heart was brimming over with it for him in that moment. It was impossible to say no. So I didn't. And there, on the rock slab, under the hot summer sun and overlooking the ocean, Toshi held my face and kissed me.

Chapter Five

Consciousness first came back to me as a bright white light and the feeling of spiraling downward in wide lazy circles. The next feeling was of an empty stomach. My vision returned and every anxiety and question came flooding back to me. A bird's brain is a small thing, so how was it that mine could be so packed full of crashing thoughts and wonderment? The angular shadows, artificial lights, and squared off parks of a city took shape beneath me. I could only hope that it was Kyoto. It wasn't like I could put GPS coordinates into the Æther.

If this city was not Kyoto, then I was in for a challenge. I had no money and no phone until I made it to the lockbox Daichi had prepared. If I was in Tokyo or Hiroshima, I would have to figure out which direction to fly in and wing there without using the Æther.

What came into view beneath me was nothing like the Japan of my childhood. Clusters of high rises and the sounds of traffic and voices formed a dense audio-fog in a layer that hung over the city.

I had also lost all sense of time while I was riding the Æther. I had to trust that I had arrived within the time frame that the wakizashi was on display.

Once I'd dropped below the roof of the tallest building, I changed into the form of a gray pigeon, small and unremarkable. I felt the weight of my silk collar more at this size, and it brushed the fronts of my wings as I flew, making my flight awkward. I dropped and flew lower, my tiny lungs protesting at the change in air quality. I needed to find somewhere I could change without being noticed.

Spying an open-air mall, I perched on the rafters of a half-roof. Lots of other birds sang and flew among the rafters, helping to camouflage me and my strange silk scarf. I hopped along the beam, my little head cocking this way and that. A large discount clothing merchant had long tables loaded with piles of mismatched merchandise. Four curtained off changing rooms marked each corner of the store. Bingo.

I flitted high over the tops of the single person changing rooms, three of which were in use. Quick as lightning, before anyone noticed a pigeon with a black silk collar around its neck, I dropped into the empty one. The feeling of a thousand stars shimmered over my body as I phased and landed on human feet. I yanked the curtain shut and untied my silk kimono. Putting it on, I wrapped it tightly around me. The robe didn't offer any more thickness than a nightie, but at least it covered me from neck to just above my knees. In its own way, it was oddly flattering, and could even be quite pretty if paired with heels. But it was definitely not the kind of outfit that people wore out and about on a regular day. I fished in the pocket at my hip for the silk slippers. They offered no actual protection for my feet, but at least they'd draw a little less attention than bare feet would.

I took a breath and opened the curtain, praying that no one would notice that I didn't have any clothing with me to try on. I wandered along the tables slowly, pretending to shop but scanning any signage I could find. Nothing gave me a clue as to where I was.

I left the discount tables and walked casually through the mall, trying to look like I belonged there. I got a few strange looks, a few stares, and some looks of concern, mostly from older women—mothering types wondering what this young girl was doing wandering around the mall in a thin black kimono. The cold of the marble floors made my feet feel cool, which cooled my whole body. Suddenly painfully conscious that I had no underclothes on, I crossed my arms over my chest. I had to get to my lockbox, and fast. This was much more uncomfortable than I'd anticipated.

I spotted a soft-cheeked woman scrolling on her cell phone and sitting on a bench by herself. "Excuse me," I said.

She looked up. As she registered what she was seeing, her eyebrows pulled together with concern, then fear.

"I'm not begging," I said, putting my hand up. "I don't want anything from you. I'm just wondering," I tucked a stray hair back behind my ear, "am I in Kyoto?"

Her brows jumped from fearful to surprised. "You don't know where you are? Are you okay?"

"Yes, I just need to get to a storage facility behind a post office in Kyoto. It's in the Hayashi district. Do you know if I am close?"

"I don't know that area," she said. "But you are in Kyoto." She took a deep breath and a thoughtful look came over her face. She inhaled through her nose with more intention this time, leaning forward toward me as she did so. Was she smelling me? That strange scent that Toshi had loved so much?

"Thank you," I said, and turned away.

"Wait," she said. "Would you like me to put the address into my GPS for you?"

My heart leapt with gratitude. When I turned back to her, her face looked completely different to when I had first approached her. The concern had melted away and she looked eager to help. "Would you?" I practically sighed with gratitude.

"Of course," she said. She slid down the bench and patted the space beside her.

I sat down and gave her the address. I peered at her phone and noticed the date on her phone. July 5. Shock jolted through me. I had ridden the Æther for a dozen days. I should be dehydrated, starving, and unable to move. But I felt good, energized even. Was the time indicative of the way Æther travel would always be? Or was it indicative of the deadline of my task? Questions I wished I had someone to ask.

"There you are," she said, holding the phone so I could see the screen. A blue line on the map appeared, showing that I was less than ten kilometers away.

"Looks like there is a train," she said, scrolling. "No, there are three trains you could take to get there."

"Would you mind zooming out?" I asked.

She pinched the screen to zoom out so I could see the layout of the city.

"A little more, please?"

She gave me a strange look, but did as I asked.

I could now see the shape of the Kyoto harbor and which direction I had to fly.

"Thank you, you've been so helpful," I said. I had enough information to get me closer.

"That's all you need?" she said, her brow wrinkling. "Not the train schedule?"

I smiled. "No, but thank you just the same." I got up.

"Okay, good luck." Her voice was doubtful.

I felt her eyes on my back as I made my way toward the discount store. With no money and no phone and no ID, my only option was to fly.

I went back to the changing booth at the open market and was winging my way over the city once again within a few minutes.

"ID please," said the gruff man behind the desk at the storage facility.

I swallowed hard and my heart began to pound. "My grandfather, Daichi, he sent you my thumbprint as identification. I shouldn't need to present you with paperwork. We chose your facility because of your state-of-the-art ID system." I hoped this was flattering to him. If he insisted on an ID card, I was screwed.

He frowned, and slid his chair close to the computer on his desk. "Last name?"

I told him for a second time. The seconds ticked by and I began to sweat, and not just from the warm summer afternoon.

"Here we are," he said. "You are right. Fingerprint ID." He shoved a small black box with a transparent panel on the top toward me. "Right hand."

I gave him my right hand and he took my thumb and pressed it to the panel, rolling it from one side to the other. A blue line of light rolled across the panel.

He nodded, satisfied. "Door to the right of you," he gestured. "You know your code? If you don't then there is nothing I can do to help you," he warned.

"Yes. I know it."

A metal door clicked and swung open and I went through. A long hallway of small lockers stretched out under fluorescent lights. I found the box and put in the code.

Relief flooded my limbs as the door popped open and I retrieved my backpack. I opened it and rifled through the contents. Cell phone (dead), cash (more than I felt safe carrying), photo ID, passport, sneakers, two changes of clothing, bank card to a bank I didn't recognize. Something crackled and I dug deeper and retrieved an energy bar. I smiled. Daichi could be thoughtful when he wanted to be.

Listening for movement on the other side of the door, I decided it was worth the chance. I hid around the corner of a stand of lockboxes, took off my silk robe and yanked on underwear, the twill pants, a bra and a t-shirt. I was just pulling on the canvas sneakers when the door opened and a voice called, "Girl? You finished?"

"Yes," I answered. I zipped my backpack shut and pulled it over my shoulder, my mouth dry. "All done." I appeared around the corner and left the locker-room as the man stood aside and held the door open for me. His eyes swept me from head to toe, noticing my change of clothes.

I ignored his look of curiosity. "Can you tell me if there is a hotel nearby?"

"Soiko Hotel," he grunted. "Two blocks." He jerked his head indicating the direction. "Can't miss the lights."

I thanked him and left, hitting the ground running.

* * *

Soiko was by no means a luxury hotel, and my room was more of a pod with barely enough room to stand. But it had outlets, a bottle of water, a clean single bed, and a wifi connection.

I plugged in my phone, kicked off my shoes and grabbed the water. I guzzled the entire thing and then collapsed backward onto the bed. I was tired, but considering how far I'd traveled, I felt remarkably good. I was in the right city, I'd retrieved my stuff, and I was within the time frame that the sword was still on display. So far so good.

For the first time since I left Canada, my thoughts went to my girlfriends. As if it could read my mind, my cell phone chirped with messages for so long I wondered if it would ever stop. All of them were between Targa, Georjayna, and Saxony.

Skimming the messages and photos that came through, I saw that they'd each arrived safely and were already embroiled in relationships and adventure. I smiled as I read Saxony's descriptions of the children she was looking after, and how she'd already met a cute Italian man named Raf. Targa had sent through jaw-droppingly gorgeous photos of a red-brick mansion covered in ivy, and choppy gray seas with golden sand beaches. From Georjayna, the image of a tall, dark and handsome man carrying a bunch of broken windows against what looked like a garage. Jasher, she explained, was drop-dead gorgeous, and also a complete troll. Even the bad news made me smile. My friends were safe, cared-for, and having the kinds of adventures teenage girls were supposed to have.

I considered texting the girls but decided to delay it until after I had the wakizashi. Questions were not something I had time or energy for at the moment. I tapped out an email to let Daichi know that I had arrived and was checked into the hotel.

I looked up the museum on the map. I could take a high-speed train into the city center and go on foot from there. With any luck, the wakizashi could be in my possession by tomorrow. How I was going to go about stealing it, I had no idea. I'd have to formulate a plan when I knew what I was dealing with.

I took a shower in the world's tiniest bathroom, brushed my teeth, and crawled into bed naked and clean. As my eyes drifted closed, the faces of my friends faded away and other faces took their place. Toshi, Aimi, my parents. I was back in Japan, back home. Only it didn't feel remotely like home, and my parents and my fiancé were long-dead and buried. And Aimi? Was she still alive? Had she and Toshi had a good life together, or had she betrayed him or used him the way some Kitsune were known to do?

Chapter Six

Toshi wasn't completely right about it being easy to convince our parents that we were perfect for one another. A few days after our secret engagement, his father came to visit my father.

Like us, Kito was descended of samurai-class and after studying tool-making under a master in Hiroshima, he was now one of the few remaining swordsmiths working under the Nihonto Tanrenkai, Japan's newly formed sword and forging society. Toshi worked as one of his sakite, an assistant. Kito was respected in Furano, Tottori, and beyond the Tottori Prefecture—as far away as Kobe and Kyoto.

My mother ushered Aimi and me out the back while the men lit their pipes and settled in for a man-to-man discussion of dowries and family alliances.

"And don't you dare eavesdrop at the windows. I'll know if you are there," my mother whispered as she sent us away. She didn't mean eavesdropping in human form. Aimi and I were notorious for taking our creature shapes so we could hide and listen to the adults talk. Mother had finally caught me when I had forgotten that birds do not look from one human to another while they are in conversation, following along with each speaker. Aimi would never have made such a mistake, but she had been a fox before she'd ever been a human, and I was a human who was trying to figure out how to be a bird.

I protested my mother's kicking us out but she would have none of it. My skin felt clammy with anxiety and my stomach threatened to bring up my lunch of steamed fish and rice. Toshi's father Kito was a fierce man, a man I knew to be good and strong, but also to be hard and determined to have his own way. What if he had found fault with me? It was irrational. Toshi's father would have barely known I existed until Toshi, or Toshi's mother on his behalf, brought me to Kito's attention.

"Come on, Akiko," Aimi said, taking my hand and pulling me toward the path that led down to the sea. "Don't worry. We know what the outcome will be."

"We do?" I asked, my voice trembling. I craned my neck, looking back at the light in the windows of our home, tempted to take wing and find somewhere to perch in a rafter or just outside the shutters.

"Of course. Why else would Kito have come unless it was to arrange a marriage for his son. Let's go swimming. It will distract you." Aimi picked a piece of long grass as we passed through the woods toward the ocean.

"I don't feel like swimming." In point of fact I felt like vomiting.

We walked in silence down to the beach where huge boulders lay scattered along the coast like some giant had long ago abandoned a game of marbles. Aimi scrambled up on one of the biggest ones, lifting her skirts high enough to expose her long pale legs. I climbed up after her, the smaller of the two of us. We sat down on the stone, warm from the sun. Aimi began to peel the grass into small green curls, whittling it down to a filament. She regarded me with her strange, moss-colored eyes. "You used to hate Toshi."

"I never hated him," I said. "He was mischievous and annoying, but I never hated him. Besides, he is not that little boy any longer."

She raised her eyebrows and gave me a sly look. "No, he's not." Her tone was pregnant with meaning. This was my

Aimi. Everything she said meant more than just the words she spoke. Innuendo was her playground.

I whacked her softly on the leg and almost smiled, but I felt too much worry to smile.

"You are not the only person in our village to notice," she said. "There are plenty of girls who like Toshi, girls who have spent the last few years not ignoring him, like you have." This was Aimi's way to bring some thought into my head that had not arrived there on its own.

"Who likes him?" I said, sharply. That day on the rock slab, there had been no doubt in my mind how Toshi felt about me, and I him. But now, doubt began to creep in.

Aimi canted her head and gazed at me without answering. Her eyebrows crept slowly up her forehead.

"You?" I blinked with surprise. "You never said."

She shrugged. "The eligible men in our village have black hearts. All except for Toshi and his father. They are the only good ones."

"All?" My head jerked back in surprise. "That can't be true." My mind skittered over the young unmarried men in our village, calling their faces up in my memory. It was the good-looking ones who came to mind first, fine faces with strong bones and good teeth. "What about Mitsuo, and Soichi, and Yuji."

"Mitsuo has the emotional construct of a beetle, Soichi is a pervert and a liar, and don't talk to me of Yuji. He's a pirate, all he cares about is money. He would step on his own grandmother's face if he thought it would get him favor with his rich uncle."

My jaw went slack at the conviction in her voice. "How do you know all this?"

She laughed. "Little sister, I am a creature of the Æther. I can see into their hearts and the rot that lives there."

"I'm a creature of the Æther, too. Why can't I see it?"

"You will," she said, tossing the curls of grass into the waves and crossing her legs under her. "Give it time."

"And you can see into Toshi's heart?"

"I can," she said, looking at me unblinking.

"What does it look like?"

"Toshi's heart is a rare white pearl," she said. "It glimmers with all the colors of the rainbow. Light pours down from the Æther and into him as though filtering first through a crystal." Whenever she talked like this, I would stare hard at her, trying to winkle out whether she was playing with me or not. "There is only one other heart that is more beautiful."

"Whose is that?"

"Yours," she said, smiling at me in her crooked way, her fox's eyes unblinking.

I shoved at her shoulder. "This isn't funny. If you liked Toshi, why didn't you ever say anything to me?"

"It's not up to me who Toshi marries," she replied. "You know that as well as I."

I frowned. "So you would marry him if our father and Kito agree you are a better match?" Bright green jealousy oozed from my heart at the very thought of Toshi marrying anyone else, especially my sister.

"Like I said, Toshi is a good man. The best to be had," Aimi answered, her voice sly.

"Ugh," I groaned. "This is not a time to talk in circles. Would you agree or wouldn't you?"

"Who am I to deny our parents?" She shrugged.

"Don't do that," I said, picking up a pebble and whipping it into the ocean.

"What?"

"Pretend that you're subject to the laws of humans. You are Kitsune, you don't have to do anything anyone tells you to do. You could disappear tomorrow and start a whole new life somewhere else, with someone else, if you wanted to."

"And leave all this? Our parents? You?" She was still avoiding answering my question. This was her nature. Aimi was as evasive as she was beautiful, as crafty as she was swift. She just didn't often turn her prevaricating ways on me. I enjoyed watching her ply them on others, but I had thought of myself as immune until now. "Come on," she said, sliding down off the rock and splashing into the shallow waves. She waded through the water to the beach.

"Where are you going?" I got up and walked along the tops of the rocks to reach the sand. She strode across the beach away from me, her dark head bobbing as the sand got deeper. "Aimi," I huffed after her.

Her dark head of hair rippled and disappeared, her dress collapsed into a heap on the sand. A big lump moved under the mess of fabric, trying to find an exit.

I sighed. "I hate when you do that. You know I'm the one who will get stuck washing your dirty clothes." As the younger sister, my tasks were the most menial ones.

A glossy blue-black fox the size of a large dog shook off the dress and looked over her shoulder at me, her tongue lolling out as she laughed. Her eyes were as bright as limes and her sharp teeth gleamed white. She flicked her tail and darted up the beach, over a moss-covered log and into the bush.

I lifted my hands out to the side, pulled my arms rapidly into through the wide arm-holes of my robe, my body shimmering like a mirage in the desert. Wings, feathers, talons and impossibly sharp eyesight took the place of my soft human body as I phased into a kintail – a small but nimble bird of prey.

I snatched at my dress before it hit the ground, carrying it in my talons to drape it over a dry rock. I picked up Aimi's dress, laid it beside mine, and winged over the woods, my kintail scream letting my sister know that the hunt was on.

The woods had gone as quiet as a tomb. The presence of a large predator had silenced every rodent, bird, and nearby deer. Animals didn't know the difference between a fox and a Kitsune. Aimi had no interest in stalking and killing prey, not anymore. But as a girl Aimi weighed nearly a hundred-twenty pounds, and when she chose to take her full size as a fox, she was enormous. Large enough to give even another predator pause to attack her. She was solid blue-black with soft thick fur and a ruff around her neck. She was nearly impossible to spot when she hid in shadows. Her mistake was looking up at the sun to watch for me. The light would reflect in her bright green eyes and my raptor's vision could find her as I soared overhead.

My shadow skimmed over the tops of our thick rainforest as I winged for the gorge. A small river gurgled over stones and fallen trees, rolling its way to the sea. The rubble of years of old avalanches had built haphazard natural stairs along the canyon. My head cocked as the sound of toenails scraping over stones echoed up to me. I banked left where a fissure in the rock met the river.

From my vantage point I could see what Aimi could not, that the space between the rock walls ahead of her narrowed to barely a hands-width and she was flying toward it at full speed. My little heart leapt into my throat and I screamed a warning cry. She didn't slow down and I called again. She sped up.

She hurtled toward the narrow gap, her black form shimmering into a fox the size of a kitten. She passed through the opening, her pelt skimming the rocks, and landed on the paws of a normal sized animal, smaller than her original shape. Aimi's unique fox-laugh bounced off the canyon walls, sounding like it was coming from everywhere.

Screaming my applause and relief, I dipped lower as the running fox disappeared under an overhanging ledge and continued through the fissure, scrabbling over stones and then sliding into the trees like a ghost.

I slowed and spiraled, catching an updraft and taking it higher. The fissure ended and became thick forest over steadily rising ground. The landscape turned into a sea of bright treetops and dark shadows. I dove down and into the trees. Here, there was no gliding, here there was only quick banks and turns. Skimming through narrow openings between branches to grab the breeze, and skipping up with it like an athlete sprinting upstairs.

A clearing bathed in sunlight up ahead revealed my prey. Aimi let loose that laugh again and I responded with a haunting scream. The race was on. She sprinted full out and I followed from above, diving and turning and trying my best not to misjudge and crash. The forest got tighter and tighter, the branches skimming my feathers. Aimi's running form appeared and disappeared below me in flashes through gaps in the canopy. We exploded into a clearing and I dive bombed for her head.

She was too quick. Bunching her hindquarters, she took a flying leap to meet me in the air. She shimmered, taking on her full-sized shape and punting me in the breast with her nose. I bounced up into the air in a turmoil of feathers, that yipping laughter coming from everywhere. I righted and circled the clearing, screaming in pretend frustration.

Aimi sat on her haunches and watched me, those bright eyes blinking into the sun, her tongue lolling out and her sides heaving. She'd won and we both knew it. She lowered onto her elbows as I flew low enough to raise the dust in front of her. She dropped her chin onto the dirt as I landed and bounced up to her. I ruffled my feathers and shook the ache out of my wings.

The sound of a human voice in the distance made Aimi raise her head and cock an ear upward. Our mother. Aimi made eye contact with me and stopped panting, going as still as a statue. I bobbed my head twice and took to the air. It took mere minutes for me to retrieve our clothing, but as I grasped the robes I realized they were too heavy for my current form. I shifted into a falcon so I could bear the burden.

I winged back to Aimi with our clothing but I deposited her dress on a branch and out of her reach. She lowered her head and watched me as I shimmered and took on my human form, pulling my dress on in front her.

She let out a whine.

I grinned at her. "You know what I want," I said. "You won that one, but unless you want to show up at home stark naked then you know what to do."

She whuffed at me, rolling her eyes and shaking her head. Her fur rippled like a sharp wind had blown over her and her big powerful form melted away, leaving a fox pup.

"Ohhhhhhh," I squealed.

She sat back on her little haunches and howled to the sky, the cry turning into a yipping laugh. Her eyes had gone the soft green of winter moss. Her ears had thickened and shrunk, soft little triangles poking out to the sides. Her fur was fuzzy and stuck out in every direction like black dandelion fluff. Her tail was short and narrow, unlike the thick bottle-brush tail of her full-grown form. It stuck up behind her and curled over to one side.

"Gaaaaa! You're so cute!" I cried.

She tottered toward me on baby fox legs and I scooped her up and held her warm body under my chin. Her fur was down-soft and hot from the sun. She licked my face and neck as I cradled her. She stuck her cold wet nose into my ear and I laughed. Kitsune rarely had reason to take the form of a kit. It was an act of love. When we were like this, I had no anxiety in the whole world and she could feel it. She stopped licking me and cocked her head, pointing her nose toward home. She gave a little whine. I hadn't heard anything with my human ears, but I knew Mother must be calling again.

"Yes, all right," I said, putting her down and climbing the tree to retrieve her robes. When I turned back to her, Aimi was in human form again and holding out her hand for her clothing.

She was shaking her head at me, a sly smile playing about her lips. "Your flying has gotten so much better," she said as she wrapped herself up and tied her dress closed. She scraped her disheveled hair back and twisted it up, retrieving a stick from her pocket to secure it.

"Still didn't win," I said.

She shrugged. "You probably will when it really counts."

I opened my mouth to ask her about her cryptic words but she spoke first.

"Shall we take the bridge back?" She began jogging for home, her bare feet flashing at me to keep up.

Chapter Seven

My mother had the door open and was waiting for us as we came up the walk, out of breath. Her brows drew together and the corners of her mouth pulled down. Her gaze traveled from the tops of our disheveled heads to our muddy feet. She shook her finger at us. "You're filthy again. You are lucky Kito has gone or he would change his mind. You couldn't pick another day to play your bush games?"

We were used to her admonitions about our sport. My mind snagged the important thing like a burr to wool. "There has been an agreement?" I asked as she ushered us inside the house.

"There has," she said. "Baths for both of you, and wash your hair. Kito returns tonight."

I bit off a groan. Preparing a bath was my job and it took a long time to heat pot after pot of water and fill the large wooden tub we kept behind the frosted sliding glass doors.

"I'll help you," Aimi said as my mother left us to talk with our father in the other room. We watched as she slid the door shut between the two rooms and gave us a stern eye to do as we were told. She and father would keep their voices so low that we wouldn't be able to eavesdrop, not in human form anyway.

Aimi allowed me to have the first bath, a luxury that, as the youngest of the family, I had never had before.

I scrubbed myself all over with wet soap first, and then sank into the steaming water with a sigh. Scratches on my legs that I hadn't noticed now stung from the hot water. I lifted my hair over the back of the tub and let my neck relax as Aimi picked the tangles out of my long black strands.

I looked up at her as she was working. From the angle I saw her at, her face upside down, her lips looked downturned and sad. My heart gave a confused pang. I wanted Toshi, more than anything, but I hated to see Aimi unhappy. "You are the eldest," I pointed out. "It is traditional to marry off the older sister first." I could barely keep my voice from hitching.

Her eyes flashed to mine. "How many elder sisters are Kitsune? Would you knowingly agree to marry a Kitsune off to a prominent member of your community without their knowledge?"

"You could bring great fortune," I said.

"I could bring great misfortune, as well. Even I don't fully know the nature of the warrior whose blood did this to me."

"Yes we do," I said fiercely, sitting up and sloshing water over the side.

"Shhh," she said, putting a hand on my shoulder and pushing me back down.

"You are a Zenko; it is impossible to think otherwise," I said, my face flushing with heat. I couldn't tell if it was from the indignation I felt when Aimi talked like this, or from the steaming tub. There were two main kinds of Kitsune, and Zenko was the benevolent kind. It was unthinkable that Aimi was the malevolent kind, known as Nogitsune.

Aimi swept my hair to the side. "Move down."

I moved forward and tilted my head back as she scooped up water with a jug and poured it over my hair. I closed my eyes with the pleasure of her fingers scrubbing at my scalp.

"When you talk like that, you sound like you want it to be me," Aimi said.

"No," I answered. "You know that I love him. You don't love him." When she didn't answer I opened my eyes and straightened my head to turn and look at her. Water ran in rivulets down my face. I rubbed them away. "Do you?"

She dumped another jug of water over my head and I had to close my eyes and cover my face.

"Do not worry about me, little sister."

Sitting there in that tub, my hands over my face and water sluicing over my head, my mind raced over the possible outcomes. Would our father knowingly wed a Kitsune into another family? Kitsune were as complex as the warriors they came from, never all good or all bad. Legends circulated of Zenko, benevolent Kitsune who healed the sick and provided wealth to families who were in great debt, who influenced events to turn in their families' favor. But there were just as many legends of Nogitsune, Kitsune who tricked people out of all of their wealth and disappeared without a trace, even of leading a husband they'd become tired of into a trap that would result in his ruin. Aimi had become my parents' daughter before I was born; I couldn't picture life without her. Father was the one who had brought Aimi in, taking the risk of inviting a nogitsune into his home. Our mother had told our father that Aimi had gifted me with a tamashī—the spiritual heart of a creature of the Æther. I was also an Akuna Hanta, a hunter of demons. What that meant for my future, I didn't know, and even Aimi seemed unable to prepare me completely.

The water stopped coming and I opened my eyes. Aimi took a bar of soap scented with yuzu oil and rubbed it into a wet cloth. She began to scrub my arm, keeping her eyes on her work, her face impassive. The truth that we both knew was that in this situation, one scenario was just as likely as another.

I put my hand over hers and she stopped scrubbing. Her green eyes met my gold and there we locked, the sisterhood we'd shared up until this moment in time as visible to me as it was to her.

"Promise me," I said, my voice shaking, "that no matter who has been given to Toshi, we will never let it come between us. We will always be sisters, always be together."

Aimi held my gaze, and the soapy washcloth stilled on my shoulder. "Akiko," she said. "You are not a little girl anymore. At some point you have to stop living in a dream world. You know that I cannot promise you this, and you cannot promise it to me either."

I gasped at the brutality of her words. She'd said them so softly, almost sweetly, but they shot straight to my heart and punctured me like a barb tipped with poison.

"No," I said, my eyes widening.

She dropped the washcloth in the tub, her expression melting. She took my cheeks in her hands. "I do not say this to hurt you, little sister. You will come into your Hanta powers soon. I will have to move on with whatever comes into my nature to do." Her voice took on a sound like wind. It blew around me and through me. "We are immortals. Forever stretches out in front of us. It is foolish to think that we can spend all of time together."

"Why?" My vision blurred as tears filled my eyes. Aimi was going to leave me? I didn't know how to be anything without her.

"Hush now," she said, releasing my face. She kissed my cheek and retrieved the washcloth from the tub. "Mother comes."

"Aimi, are you in the tub yet?" came our mother's voice.

"Just getting in now, Mother," she said.

"You are dawdling." We heard the sounds of her hands clapping together, the way she did when she was trying to hurry us along.

"Yes, Mother," Aimi and I said at the same time.

Aimi brushed a tear away from my cheek, smiled at me, and picked up the jug to rinse me. "Cheer up. We have a fiancé to meet."

Kito arrived without Toshi and as I stood there behind my parents with my eyes on the floor, disappointment curdled in my stomach. I had thought there was a chance he would come.

Aimi and I stood side by side, our hair pulled back and up in the traditional hairstyle of Furano, our village. We wore our best kimonos—Aimi striking in a moss-green that flattered her eyes, and me in my favorite shade of blue, like the sky on a cloudless day.

There was bowing all around as my father, dwarfed by Kito's stature, welcomed him into our home. "These are my daughters, Aimi—the eldest, and Akiko. Good girls, both of them." My father's chest puffed out at these words and my mother's face colored. She wouldn't say so in Kito's company, but my mother's advice was always to project humility.

"Truly, you did not do your daughter's beauty justice," Kito said, in a voice that was surprisingly soft.

My eyes flashed up to Kito and back down to the floor. My heart plummeted. His eyes had been on Aimi with these words.

"Had I been given daughters and not sons, I would be thankful for girls such as these," Kito said. His shadow fell over me as he stood in front of me. “Don’t be afraid to look me in the eye.”

I looked up and my eyes made contact with his. Gray, with a ring of brown around the pupil. My neck ached at the angle it needed to take to look up at him.

I fought the urge to squirm under his scrutiny. I clutched at my forearms under the sleeves of my kimono, trying to warm my ice-cold hands.

"You are very small," Kito said.

I said nothing. A woman who was too small was not as desirable in the rural areas like ours. Our family was descended of the samurai class, which was my saving grace. I would never be required to take on the back-breaking labor of a farmer's wife, but the job of child-bearing fell to every woman, and the bigger, stronger women could bear more babies and would be more likely to have big boys.

"Toshi tells me you esteem one another, is this true?" he asked, his eyes darting around my face in search of the truth.

My lips parted to answer but my father got there first. "Akiko is the youngest, it is Aimi we agreed to this morning." His voice was gentle, wanting to correct the mistake without embarrassing Kito.

"I know," replied Kito, his eyes never leaving mine. "What do you say, girl?"

My heart pounding so loud in my ears it nearly drowned out my own voice, I found my courage. My father *had* offered Aimi, not me. This might be my only chance to fix it.

"I do not just esteem your son," I said, my voice trembling. "I love and respect him." My voice grew stronger at the look of pleasure on Kito's face. "I would follow him anywhere, give him many children, and use any resource at my disposal to further his position."

"Akiko," my mother said quietly, admonishing me.

"No, I like a girl who can speak her mind when asked." Kito stepped back. "I am a descendant of an onna-bugeisha. I know the value that it is possible for a woman to bring, and the men of our age ignore this at their peril. I want a wife with a spirit like Tomoe Gozen for my son."

"If I might," Aimi spoke, and Kito's eyes tracked to her. "I believe I am a better match for your son. I am older, stronger, wiser in the ways of our village politics, and able to counsel Toshi into a place of great respect."

"This is most unusual," my father said, bewildered. The situation had gone in a direction that none of us had expected. Daughters were never asked for their opinions.

Kito turned toward Aimi. "Are you saying Toshi would be undeserving of this respect without you at his side?"

Aimi hesitated. "No, of course not. I meant no offense. Only that I can offer Toshi something more."

My eyes were on the floor, but I didn't need to look at her to know what she was trying to convey. I could tell from the tone of her voice. She'd apologized, but her voice was loaded with secrets. Aimi was Kitsune, a creature of power, capable even of nudging fate if she felt inclined. She was a being that humans with a taste for risk tried to trap and enlist to their cause.

But I was a creature of the Æther, too, capable of... and there my thoughts stalled. Capable of what? That was the problem, I didn't know yet. Anger filled my mouth with bitterness, but my fear was stronger. Aimi was attempting to sway Kito's preference with words. How far would she go? Would she use her power to alter this outcome into her favor? I turned my head to look at Aimi, but she kept her gaze on Kito.

Kito made a long thoughtful grunt in the back of his throat. "But you do not love him."

Aimi opened her mouth to respond when Kito raised a hand. "More importantly, he does not love you." He turned away from both of us. "Excuse me for this unexpected turn of events, Okaasan. I exchanged words with my son this afternoon." Kito dropped his chin on his chest, thoughtfully. "I speak of love but I am no sentimental fool. I was once in a similar position. I know the value of true affection. I would have a wife for my son who sees him the way my wife sees me. If you are not opposed—"

My father was appeased by this show of deference. He nodded. "I am not against the match."

The two men grasped forearms and it was finished.

My mother ushered us from the room as the men discussed a few details. My legs trembled and I thought for a moment I would collapse. It had not yet sunk in. Was I really to be Toshi's bride?

When we were in the bedroom Aimi and I shared, my mother glared at both of us. "Not another word until he leaves," she said under her breath. She slid our door shut and left Aimi and I standing there alone.

I felt out of breath. A confusion of emotions threaded their way through me. Elation at the outcome, anger with Aimi, but also a cold rationalization. I might have done the same thing had I been in her shoes. After all, our father had chosen her for Toshi, not me. In a way, I had stolen him from her.

Aimi knelt down and crawled onto her sleeping platform. Without bothering to take off her kimono, she lay down on her side facing the wall.

With some difficulty, I changed into my sleeping shift, put away my kimono, and went to my own bed. I lay down with my back to her.

Chapter Eight

The Ryozen Museum was an L-shaped, two-story building nestled among green shrubs and graced with elegantly curved, pagoda-inspired roofs. It did not look like a place with state-of-the-art security, which made me feel a little better, but the weight of what I was about to do still pressed heavily on me. Inside this building lay the key to my freedom. All I had to do to have my tamashī back was steal an antique short sword.

I stood on the street looking up at the museum entrance. In my purse was a color printout of the blue wakizashi in its sheath. It wasn't great quality but it was the best I could get from a frozen video screenshot.

My heart pounded in my ears, blocking out the sound of footsteps, conversation, honking, and traffic.

Daichi had never asked me to steal for him before. And in my life before Daichi captured my tamashī, I had never stolen. My parents had raised me to keep my hands off things that weren't mine. Now I was going to steal from the state, from my country, from this museum, and from the Japanese people—my people.

I took a deep breath to settle my nerves and walked up the steps to the entrance. I passed through the doors and approached the ticket booth. The noise of the street was shut out and the sound of my footsteps was muffled by a strip of carpet leading to a set of turnstiles.

"Ticket for one, please," I said to the woman working at the booth. I paid four hundred yen for my ticket and inserted it into the turnstile. I passed through the metal bar and went inside. The museum was impeccably clean and quiet. Banners hung on the walls advertising displays.

I took a pamphlet from a stand behind the turnstile and opened it out to see a map. Displays were unhelpfully labeled 'Men Who Changed Japan,' and 'Shoguns at Tokugawa's End.' I frowned. Nothing on the map directed me to where I would find swords. A silent wander down a carpeted hall lined with glass display boxes had me chewing my lip nervously. Anything of value was enclosed behind glass, and the artifacts had not been organized by category but by year. Daichi had not given me any clue as to how old the wakizashi was, so it seemed as though I would have to comb every display to find it.

My eyes tracked the curved shapes of katanas – the long samurai swords, and wakizashi, but they were few and far between. I kept wandering, keeping my pace slow and my face serene. If there was video in this place, it wouldn't help to have me recorded as rushing from sword to sword.

I took my time and combed every display with the thorough eye of a sleuth. Only when I was satisfied that the blue sheathed wakizashi was not on the ground floor level did I head for the second floor.

Hushed voices reached my ears from the upper level and I took the stairs at the end of the display. A few couples stood near the glass cases, discussing the artifacts in front of them. A woman in a museum uniform stood near the top of the stairs. I nodded to her as I passed, holding my ticket where she could see it. She gave me a polite smile.

I passed a rusting metal shell from the Boshin War and stopped to read the label, playing the interested citizen. I moved on slowly, taking in the art, armor, and reading the stories, making my way toward the entrance to the next room and the only display I hadn't yet combed. I passed through the doorway. A man with a white beard in a janitor's uniform bumped my shoulder as he walked by me.

"Excuse me," I said.

He turned and said, "Pardon me."

In my periphery, I thought he stopped there in the doorway. I kept walking, my back to him. As I turned to face another display, I caught him in the corner of my eye. He *was* staring. My heart rate went up a notch. I did my best to ignore his probing eyes.

My anxiety grew as I moved along. The short sword didn't seem to be on the upper level either. I examined the map to be certain that I hadn't missed any of the displays. I walked back and forth so many times I lost count.

Our wakizashi was not here.

My fingers felt ice cold and I shoved my hands into my pockets to warm them. Daichi and I hadn't discussed what we would do if the sword wasn't here. I chewed my lip, my mind racing. I would have to ask the museum staff. What else could I do? It would damn me later, but by the time they put my seemingly innocent request together with the missing sword, I would be long gone.

I made my way back to the woman in the museum uniform, passing by the janitor, who still seemed to be keeping an eye on me.

"Excuse me?" I smiled as I approached her.

"Yes?" She stood and stepped closer to me, pleasant, ready to help.

"I came to see a particular wakizashi..." I retrieved the printout of the weapon from my purse. "It is a really beautiful artifact and I was so hoping to see it, but I haven't been able to find it. It was in your promotional video. Can you direct me to where it is displayed?"

She pulled a pair of glasses out of the inner pocket of her jacket and put them on. She took the page and looked at it. Her smile disappeared and a line appeared between her eyes. "This sword was retrieved by its owner. I'm sorry but it's no longer part of the display." She said the words bluntly and handed the page back to me. She took a step back, removed her glasses and tucked them into her pocket. Her eyes shuttered, but not before I saw a flash of fear. She clasped her hands behind her back.

"Before the scheduled date?" I pressed. My stomach dipped with anxiety. "They were supposed to be on display for another week. I came especially to see this wakizashi."

She gave a sharp shake of her head. "I'm sorry. It can sometimes happen. We are grateful to our sponsors for allowing us to display their treasures." She sounded like an automaton. "If, for some reason, they need to retrieve their items early, that is their right. Now, if you'll excuse me."

She turned on her heel and walked briskly away, pulling the hem of her jacket down sharply.

"Wait, please," I said, following her. "Who is the owner?"

She didn't look back, and instead increased her speed and exited the display area.

Worry multiplied in my gut like a split-open sack of baby spiders, its creatures running in all directions. Her reaction was not at all normal. What had happened to the sword? Why would its owner remove it? Did they somehow know I was coming? I shook my head at this impossibility. Daichi was relying on my success; he wouldn't tell anyone of our plans, and I couldn't have spilled our plot even if I had wanted to.

Movement caught my eye. The janitor appeared in the doorway behind me. His expression was so strange, like he was trying hard to recognize me, like he thought I might be someone who meant something to him once. We stared at each other. I studied his face, but no, I didn't know this man. I was sure of it.

He took a few steps closer, his face going through a remarkable transformation. Curiosity to suspicion, suspicion to shock, shock to joy. He stopped a mere foot away, his upper body swaying toward me slightly. His dark eyes never left my face.

"Can I help you?" I asked. The look on his face frightened me, almost like he'd found a long-lost friend or family member.

"Akuna Hanta," he whispered. His eyebrows were up, his eyes fully alight. It was not a question. There was a surety in his face. He knew what I was.

I froze in shock, then gave a sharp intake of breath and scanned the room. The other museum patrons were locked in their own conversations and paid us no mind.

"How do you know what I am?" I whispered.

"Forgive me, I overheard your conversation with Mrs. Okina. You are looking for the wakizashi? The one with the beautiful blue sheath," he said, stepping even closer.

"Yes." My heart was drumming like the hoofbeats of a runaway horse. Alarm bells were going off in my head so loud I could hardly think. How did this man know me? My instinct told me to run, but my command told to me grab this lead with both hands. "Why, do you know where it is?"

He looked around, eyes darting about the room as though we were about to make an exchange of illegal contraband. He shoved a hand into his pocket and retrieved a crumpled receipt. He plucked a pen from his shirt pocket and scribbled something on the back of the scrap. It was then that I noticed that he was missing the end of his right pinkie finger.

"Come here. Tonight. Come alone. It is my place, and there it will be safe to talk." He shoved the crumpled paper into my hand, and dropped the pen into his pocket. He dipped a small bow. "Please. I need to help you."

"Who are you?" I asked, breathlessly. Just then another museum staff member appeared at the top of the stairs. He frowned at us. It probably looked like one of his cleaning staff was harassing a patron.

The janitor tapped his index finger on the paper. "My name is Inaba. Come tonight. For dinner." He turned away, giving a surreptitious glance at the staff member and disappearing behind a door marked *staff only*.

I opened the crumpled page. A simple address. Nothing else. I blew out a breath. *I need to help you.* Strange choice of words. Why *need*? And why was it not safe to talk here?

Chapter Nine

As Toshi and my wedding drew closer, Mother spent a lot more time with me. She taught me how to make a tea ceremony for my husband, how to manage a household, when to shop for the best cuts of meat, how to speak to the tailor to tell him how I wanted my family's clothing to fit, how to choose the best fabrics for each kind of outfit, and what a husband would expect on our wedding night. Every conversation held me in thrall, and my mother's vague description of the way babies were made left me blushing and anxiety-ridden. If the way horses and dogs did it was any indication, I wasn't so sure I was up for the duty, even with Toshi. My mother reassured me, with a pink face, that sometimes it could be simply wonderful.

One day as we walked home from the tailor after a fitting for my wedding kimono, we passed Toshi and Kito in the street going the opposite direction. Toshi had a basket fastened to his back and I could hear the clink of metal as he shifted his load. We acknowledged each other with deferential nods and continued on our way. Before Toshi passed out of my vision, I saw a big grin break out on his face and I couldn't help but smile myself.

"Stop grinning like a fool," my mother said quietly. "There are already enough young women jealous of you; you don't need to gloat." Her words were stern but her voice was gentle.

I pressed my lips together. I glanced around the street and noticed the eyes of several people on me, mostly the calculating stares of women close to my age. I hadn't been gloating, but I saw her point. "Sorry, Mama."

"My dear, Akiko," she said as we passed through the busiest part of town and the crowd began to thin. "Are you certain that marriage is what you want?"

I came to an abrupt halt, shock widening my eyes. I thought that I had heard her wrong. For young women of our time, marrying well was the ultimate achievement; there was nothing else. For my own mother to ask me if it was what I wanted was impossible, unthinkable, beyond reason.

"Mama?" was all I could manage. I was walking slightly behind her, as was our custom, and I craned my neck to see her face.

Only the side of her face was visible and she showed no signs of having made a joke. She remained silent until we arrived home.

"You are Akuna Hanta," my mother began as we boiled water for tea. "For whatever reason, the Æther has chosen to gift you with this power. Are you certain that your role in this world will be fulfilled if you marry Toshi? Or any man?"

"But I love him," I said. "I do not understand what I am to do if it is not to be a loving wife."

The look on my mother's face told me that she didn't know either, and she was at a loss for how to council me. All any mother would want for her daughter was a man like Toshi, but I was no normal daughter. She sat down across from me on the floor.

"Is this not what you want for me?" I asked, examining her face for some revelation.

"I did," she admitted. "Up until the day you first took the form of a bird, it was all I wanted for you."

I poured the hot water into our cast iron kettle and set it on the table. Pulling down two cups, I joined my mother at the table and we waited for the tea to steep.

"When your father found Aimi, she was cold, naked and hungry. She didn't know how to speak, and she had nothing and no one."

"Did Father know what she was?"

"Not at first," she said, stroking a few wisps of loose hair back from her face. "Kitsune are something that we are told about as children. They may or may not be a fairy tale, and the legends of them bringing either great fortune or great destruction to the families or men who take them in are just that, legends."

"But legends come from somewhere," I said. These were words I had heard my father say many times in the past.

Mother nodded. "Most people dismiss Kitsune as myth, your father and I included. But as we nursed Aimi back to health, and saw her intelligence and how quickly she learned to speak, we began to have our suspicions. Your father's business had been struggling and soon after taking her in, everything seemed to go right and we became much more prosperous. When I was approached by a large black fox in the garden one summer day, I knew without a doubt that I was looking at our adopted daughter. She never had to tell us in so many words, what she was. She knew when we were ready to see her in her true form, and it wasn't even a shock. Before Aimi came into our lives, marrying a daughter to someone like Kito's son would have been impossible, a dream. But after..." She trailed off.

"After, what?" I prompted her, as I picked up the teapot to pour her tea. The steaming liquid filled the air with the scent of toasted rice and greens.

She raised her eyes to mine. "Do you remember anything from when you were still in my womb?"

I blinked in surprise. "Is it possible for a baby to remember something from before their birth?"

"Not a normal child, no, I don't think so. I only ask because I have never felt anything like what I felt when Aimi gave you her blessing. It was so powerful that I thought you might have some memory of it."

I sat down across from her, the tea forgotten. "What did you feel, Mother?"

She got a faraway look in her eyes. "The only word I can think of to describe it was ecstasy," she said softly.

My breath caught in my chest for in that moment my mother's face looked as youthful as mine. It was as though just the memory of the moment was enough to erase the lines of worry that had etched themselves into her skin over the years. My mother had always been beautiful, even as she aged, but just then she was a window into the past. My body swept with gooseflesh and I was afraid to speak, afraid that it would break the spell.

"I was already eight moons and you were such an active baby. You would kick with excitement whenever Aimi laid her hand on my belly. But that day, she laid her hand on my belly and brought her face close to you. She whispered, 'For giving me a home and a family, I give your daughter a tamashī. May she take it and be blessed.'" My mother closed her eyes and a tear escaped and rolled down her pale cheek. "They were simple words. I did not know what a tamashī was, but in that moment I was overcome by a feeling of so much love. It was everywhere inside and outside of me, it erased every bad feeling and bad dream I had ever had, and filled me completely. It chased out all of my fear and anxieties, of which there were many, and I knew only rest and peace." She wiped the tear away. "I have been wishing for another small taste of that feeling ever since, and I wonder if it is what good people feel after they die." She focused on me. "When you were born, all the women of the village heard from the midwife about how easy the birth was. I didn't know what to expect, but you were just a normal baby, pink and perfect, and even your father was not disappointed that you were born a girl."

"That too, was a gift from Aimi," I said, and my mother nodded in agreement.

My mother laughed. "Your father and I were shocked beyond reason the first time you became a bird. Why you chose to become a tiny peacock to wander in our garden was beyond me."

I gave a half-smile. "I saw one at the traveling fair that came through Furano when I was six. Do you remember? I was so enchanted by it."

"Oh, is that why?" She laughed again. "I pulled Aimi aside and asked her what it meant and she was just as surprised as we were. She looked so pale and serious until she saw that it scared me and then told me not to worry. She said, 'She has taken the tamashī I gave her and become an Akuna Hanta. There is nothing false in her, for the Æther has chosen her to be one of the highest beings of its realm.'"

It was nice to hear this story, to finally know something of what had happened to make me what I was, but I felt the growing weight of expectations. Yes, I could have wings, but beyond that I was just a regular girl, unremarkable. I had never even seen an akuna, didn't even know what a demon looked like or how they affected people, how they operated.

"So," my mother interrupted my thoughts. "When I ask you if you are sure that marriage is what you want, it is with all of this in mind. Knowing that the Æther has chosen you for its purpose, and that you will be used for good in this world, who are we to commit you to the life of wife and mother?" She picked up her steaming cup and raised it to her lips.

"Maybe," I ventured, "maybe being a wife and a mother is necessary for me to grow into my Hanta powers. For what good is it to be a defender and a protector of humans against the demonic realms, if I have not had the human experience myself?"

My mother stared at me over her cup, thinking over my words. She took a sip and put her cup down. "I suspect some of your Hanta wisdom is beginning to show itself." She inclined her head in a show of deference that mothers rarely gave to their daughters. "As you wish."

Chapter Ten

"You're late," I said to Toshi as he came through the trees and into the sunlight beating down on our rock slab.

"I am sorry," he said, breathing hard from the climb. "Father has graduated me to weighing the value of the swords we turn out of our ovens. It is not as easy as you might think. I have to practice with every weapon we make before I can make an educated recommendation for price. I feel like he knows that soon I will no longer be under his roof and is trying to extract every bit of labor from me that he can."

Toshi's words could have been taken as a complaint, but his tone was good-natured. He approached and dipped his head at me politely, then swooped in and kissed my cheek.

"But you like swinging swords around," I said. "I've never seen you happier."

"My happiness has nothing to do with swordplay, I assure you," Toshi laughed. "And what has my little bird been up to these last days?"

My heart always swelled when he called me by this nickname. Toshi did not know I was a Hanta, and yet he'd chosen 'little bird' for me. I knew it was for my fine bones and tiny stature, but I liked to think it was also because he could feel my other nature in some way.

We talked and laughed until Toshi had to go. It was his duties which kept us apart more than mine. We kissed goodbye and agreed to meet again in a few days. I watched his figure retreat into the woods and then I turned back to the ocean. I sat down cross-legged in a patch of sunlight, absorbing the heat from the clifftop. Birds sang and chirped without restraint. I spotted the backs of two whales cresting in the water. Two pelicans winged overtop, so close to one another that their wings nearly touched. Every creature needed its companion. A pang went through my heart. Aimi and I had not played for weeks. We'd hardly exchanged words.

The birds had stopped singing and nothing but the sound of the wind and waves reached my ears. A light scattering of pebbles made me turn.

A blue-black fox the size of a large cat padded across the rock toward me. Aimi came closer, her head down, her mouth closed. She sat on her haunches a few feet away.

"You found me," I said. My soft words belied the excitement I felt to see my Kitsune sister on this clifftop again.

She made a show of getting up and sniffing the moss around me. She crossed behind me and sat down on my other side.

"He just left," I said.

She blew a breath out of her nose and looked out at the ocean.

"I miss you," I whispered.

Her mouth opened and her tongue appeared as she panted under the sun's heat. Those green eyes found mine and she got up and came closer. She nosed my elbow and I lifted my arm to let her in close to my side. I let my arm come to rest on her shoulders and all was right with the world again.

"You talk about us as being creatures of the Æther. What is the Æther, anyway?" I asked Aimi as we gathered flowers in the woods to fill our home with the fragrance of summer. "Mother thinks it is the place where faith lives—is that what you think, too?"

Aimi popped a violet blossom in her mouth and chewed. "I might describe it better as spirit." We moved through a thick carpet of violets, our footfalls silenced by the soft stems and flowers. "It will be different for you than for me, I think."

That drew me up and I stopped walking. "Why would it be different?"

"You are Akuna Hanta, I'm only Kistune. I'm a creature with power, but I am as flawed as any human. My motives can be selfish, or altruistic. As a Hanta, you are capable only of good."

I thought back along the timeline of my childhood: the time I cut Aimi's hair while she was sleeping, took a spoonful of honey in the middle of the night because I was hungry, and dressed up in my mother's most expensive kimono when she wasn't home, got the hem dirty and then blamed it on Aimi. "That's not true."

"Not in your human form," Aimi said with a laugh. "But when you become a Hanta, you are an agent of the gods, capable of destroying the most powerful and wicked demons. Even Oni."

I shuddered as the image of the red-skinned devil with horns and fangs and carrying a nasty looking spiked club rose to my mind. These ugly fearsome creatures were sometimes painted on room-dividers and robes as a warning. Legends told that they meted justice out to the wicked and loved to feed on human flesh. Bile rose in my throat. I had always thought the legends were contradictory. How could something that was supposed to mete out justice on the wicked be so wicked itself? It made no sense. "How am I supposed to destroy an Oni?"

"You ask so many questions, thinking I might have the answers," Aimi said patiently.

"Who else should I ask? You are the one who did this to me."

"But I didn't know you'd come out as a Hanta." Aimi turned around and looked back at me, holding her palms out. "I thought you'd just be a girl blessed with sharp intuition and good luck. It's your own heart that took my gift and made you what you are."

"A bird," I replied, crossing my arms. I dropped my chin and gave Aimi a look that said I wasn't impressed. I had always thought that Aimi had been given a superior ability to mine.

"No." Aimi raised her eyebrows in surprise and strode up to me. She put a hand on my forearm. "I mean, yes, you can become a bird, but because you're a creature of the air, you can get closer to the Æther than anyone or anything else. You can touch the sky. You can visit where all the good spirits live and where they are made. The Æther feeds power into both of us, but you're from a higher realm." At my expression of confusion, she sighed. "Have you ever tried to take the form of a vulture?"

"What?" I dropped my arms. "No, why would I?"

Aimi stepped back. "Try it. Right now. Just humor me, please."

I dropped my arms, pictured a vulture, and waited for the feeling of a thousand little stars dancing over my body as I took a winged shape.

Nothing happened.

Aimi cocked an eyebrow. "Well?"

I looked down and then back up at her, bewildered. "I can't. Why can't I?" I tried again, and failed again. Nothing changed.

"Vultures are carrion eating birds. Creatures that live on death. A fox is a predator, but it's also a scavenger and a trickster. As a Hanta, the Æther gives you the form of creatures who live in the highest realm, and who do not live on death."

"But I can take on the shape of a falcon, an owl, and a hawk. They all kill to survive."

"Yes, but the difference is that they are hunters. They take something that is alive and make it dead. Vultures feed on things that are already dead and rotting. The shapes that you can take are symbolic of your purpose. Birds hunt from the skies, you hunt from the highest realms of the spirit, combing the realms below you. Those birds hunt mice and rodents from the sky. You hunt demons. Now do you see?"

My mind spun as all this sank in. Aimi turned away and kept walking.

"So how am I supposed to hunt these demons? What do I do with them?" I stumbled after her, catching up.

"I don't know the answer to that, but I have faith that you will. When you're ready."

"When will that be?"

"When you get the Hanta vision, I guess." Aimi stooped to cut a cluster of flowers and add them to her basket. "And not a second before," she chuckled. "The Æther works that way. The answers come, but always at the last minute. It's like it is always testing how strong our faith is."

My mind went back to what Aimi had said about Toshi's heart being as beautiful as a pearl. I watched her thoughtfully. Always more graceful than me, always slightly ahead of me. She had so much faith in the Æther providing us with the knowledge we needed when we needed it. I added more blossoms to my basket and we harvested side by side in silence. Me digesting all this new information, and Aimi thinking her Kitsune thoughts. Whatever they were.

"Do you remember anything from the days before you were a Kitsune?" I asked.

"You mean from when I was just a fox?" Aimi had a basket filled with daisies draped over her arm. My basket was full of lilies. Together we would make numerous bouquets and deliver a few among our neighbors. It was something Aimi and I had done every year since I was small. "Some," she replied, bending to cut more stems. "I remember coming to a battlefield and hearing the sounds of dying men. It was their cries that attracted me in the first place."

"Do you know who had been fighting?"

"I have no idea. I had no interest, either. All I wanted was to follow my nose toward the scent of blood. I remember being very fearful of the smell of men, but also that these men were wounded and would pose less of a threat." She laughed. "Makes it sound like I was able to rationalize, but it wasn't like that. My thoughts weren't really thoughts, they were just instinct."

"What happened then?" I tucked the stem of a blossom into my hair.

She shrugged. "It's hazy, but I remember skirting the bodies until the smell of one of them drew me in. He was still alive, but he was dying, and the smell of his blood was so thick and strong."

I shuddered. "That was when you drank some?"

"Yes. But I got scared away by the sound of horses approaching. I didn't drink very much." She shrugged. "I guess the quantity doesn't matter so much."

"And you had no idea what it was going to do to you? That it was going to make you into a Kitsune?"

"Of course not," she said. "I was just a fox like any other. There was nothing special about me."

"Did you feel any different?"

"Not that I can recall," she said. "Not until I was dying."

"How much later was that?"

"Oh, years, Akiko. I lived out all of the days a fox could hope for. I was old and infirm when I died."

"The blood stayed in you all that time?"

"I don't know. I guess whatever you eat becomes a part of you in some way, and I had eaten something that gave me a tamashī. Or maybe it was the spirit of the samurai that left his body and went into mine." Aimi sat on a rock and took out our water bag. She took the kerchief from around her neck, wiped her face, and held the bag out for me.

"What is a tamashī, exactly?" I took the bag and put it to my lips for long refreshing swallows.

Aimi laughed as I sat down beside her and handed her back the bag. "You have one. Can't you feel it?"

"I don't think so." I frowned.

"Maybe because you started life as a human, so you've always had it. I started life as an animal, so when I got my tamashī, I could feel the difference." Aimi took a sip and put the bag down. "Watch."

She turned toward me, and keeping her gaze on me, she flicked her left hand out and opened her palm. A light appeared in the region of her heart, glowing under the fabric of her robe.

I gasped and leapt to my feet, staring at her chest.

The glow moved down her left arm and I followed it with my eyes as it moved along underneath her sleeve. It rolled out of her sleeve and came to rest in the palm of her hand. Its brightness almost made me squint.

"What is it?" I breathed. The small bright ball looked like a star, and it twinkled with a warm yellow light.

"It's my tamashī," she said. "My connection to the Æther and the source of my power." She closed her fist around the light, reopened it and the light was gone. "Maybe some would call it my soul."

"How did you do that? Can I do that?"

"Of course," she said. "Just try it."

I opened my left palm the same way she had. Nothing happened. I looked at Aimi.

She looked thoughtful. "Try it with your right hand."

I made the same motion with my right hand, and a light appeared in the region of my heart. I gasped and then laughed. I felt it there, warm and humming. I sent the ball of light down my right arm and into my hand. My tamashī was brighter, whiter, and larger than Aimi's. We both had to squint to look at it.

"More evidence of the difference between you and me," she murmured.

"What?" I asked, blinking at her over the light.

"The fact that it came to your right hand, not to your left." Something in her face looked sad at this. But before I could ask her to expand on this thought she said, "Just be very careful with this, little sister." She held a hand out to shield her eyes from the glare.

"Why?"

"Because it is the seat of your power, and it can be snatched—" Quick as a striking cobra she grabbed my tamashī and dashed away. "—like that!" she cried, laughing.

"Hey!" I took off after her, laughing too. "Come back, thief!"

She giggled as she darted through the trees, the soles of her shoes teasing me as she kept just out of reach. We pounded through the trails we both knew so well until Aimi darted off the path and onto rougher ground. She skimmed nimbly over the rubble and boulders between thick shrubs and thorny bushes. They grabbed at my clothing and I heard a tearing sound. I didn't care, and doubled my efforts in pursuit of her. It was the first time Aimi and I had played since my engagement to Toshi. My heart was flying with happiness.

Aimi's form disappeared up and over the edge of a boulder. When I heard her scream, my heart vaulted into my mouth and I sped up to crest the rocky rise where she had vanished from view. I pulled up in shock.

An elderly stranger stood in the small clearing, he turned toward us as we came over the rocks, Aimi first. He was holding a twisted walking staff in a gnarled hand. A bright yellow kerchief had been tied around his throat, and a matching hat sat on his head.

Aimi gave another shocked cry of surprise and lost her footing as the stones moved under her feet. She fell forward and sprawled across the rocks, crying out in pain. My tamashī spilled out of her grasp and rolled across the stones toward the man.

His wizened face blossomed with shock and his eyes widened in surprise, the light from my tamashī reflected in his pupils. He moved faster than a man of his years had right to. He grabbed the hat from his head, bent, and caught the light into it. A sigh of amazement issued from his throat as he cradled my tamashī in his hat.

In front of me, Aimi's form shimmered and she transformed into a fox. She disappeared inside her dress as her clothing collapsed into a heap. She leapt from the gaping neck, snarling and snapping at the man. He took a step back and raised his cane to strike her.

"No!" I cried.

Aimi lunged. The man brought his walking stick down hard, but Aimi bolted between the man's legs and the cane snapped in two on the rocks as she disappeared into the undergrowth. It was the violence of his blow that penetrated my heart with fear. He'd had intent to injure her.

"Aimi!" I yelled. The instinct to follow her was strong, but I couldn't leave my tamashī.

"What are you?" the man said, his voice raw and dry. Something in his face told me that he had some ideas about what we were. He'd just seen Aimi transform in front of his eyes.

I stared at him, my eyes wide as saucers. Sweat trickled down the hollow of my spine.

"That's mine." I held out my hand. "I need it back, now, please."

He took a step forward. "Are you Kitsune?" I couldn't see the light from my tamashī, closed in the cap the way it was.

I shook my head and reached for the hat. Was I going to have to tackle this man to get my tamashī back? My mouth had gone as dry as a desert and my hands trembled with adrenalin. Should I become a raptor and batter him with my wings? Snatch the hat in my talons? Just the thought was enough to transform my body. My robes fell and the shape of a peregrine falcon shot upward from the neck of my dress. In a flurry of feathers and clutching talons I climbed and gathered momentum to dive at him.

His face tilted up to watch me, his expression transforming from surprise to amazement. "Akuna Hanta," he whispered with understanding. He took a staggering step backward as I circled over his head. He gasped and opened the hat. The glow from my tamashī lit his face and the forest around both of us.

I dove, screaming a falcon's cry as I went.

He lifted my tamashī to his lips and I pulled up as I realized what he was about to do, turning my talons toward his face. I was too late. A piercing shriek tore from my throat as my light disappeared into his mouth. He ducked as my talons snapped closed where his face used to be. I swooped and shot upward again, preparing for another attack.

"Down." The command cracked through the air like thunder.

Some undeniable force pulled me down like a typhoon shoving me toward earth rather than lifting me to the heavens. I screamed in confusion and sprawled into the dirt at his feet, my wings open, my chest and beak in the soil. My whole body trembled, and I screamed again in terror. What was happening? Where was Aimi? Why was she not here to help me?

The man's shadow fell over me, and with it, a desperate cold.

"You will give me years," he said, taking off his outer robe. "Destiny has finally answered my call."

The last thing I saw before he threw his jacket over me were the green eyes of a blue-black fox watching from the underbrush. A horrible thought rose in my mind as the darkness suffocated me—that Aimi had known he was there and had lured me toward my doom. For with me out of the way, there would be nothing to stop her from marrying Toshi.

Chapter Eleven

From the hotel, I had to take the train southwest of Kyoto to a poorer suburb. The wealth of Kyoto began to dissolve as the minutes passed until I found myself looking at what could nearly be identified as slums. My heart slipped down into my shoes and I began to doubt my intuition about the janitor who had compelled me to do what I was doing. What if he was just crazy? I shook my head. He knew what I was. How many humans could tell an Akuna Hanta just from looking at them? None, in my experience, except for Daichi, but he'd seen my tamashī.

I stepped off the train at the right stop and used my GPS to make my way to the address. It was a tiny house, squashed in a row of tiny houses with not so much as an inch between them and no space between the sidewalk and the front door. The windows were blocked with white paper and a dim glow lit them from within. I stepped up and knocked.

The door opened and Inaba stood beside it, smiling, his eyes crinkling. He was dressed in a traditional Japanese robe, black with gray stripes. He wore his robe crossed high at his neck, and it struck me as odd-looking, like he'd purposefully done it up high to hide something, a necklace or a charm, perhaps. "Come in, come in, please," he said, stepping back from the door and leaving room for me to enter through the narrow doorway.

The smell of incense hit my nose and my gaze was caught on two candles burning on a shelf on the wall. Between the two candles were the photographs of two people: one was a teenage boy; he was smiling into the camera and shared the shape of Inaba's brow. The other was of a woman, unsmiling but serene, with her dark hair parted in the middle and tied back.

"I am Inaba." My host bowed to me. "I'm sorry we didn't have time for proper introductions at the museum. The supervisor is quite strict about the cleaning staff interacting with patrons."

"Akiko," I said. I followed him into the small space towards a low table.

"Please, come in Akiko. It is an honor to have you in my home, and to learn your name." Inaba sat down cross-legged at a low table and gestured for me to take the place across from him. A bowl sat at each place with another bowl placed upside down on top of it to serve as a lid. "You must have so many questions," he said. "I am not the greatest cook in the world. My wife was superb, but I'm afraid her talents did not rub off on me." He lifted the lid from his bowl. The smell of miso and onion mingled with the scent of incense. "Please, enjoy. I don't stand on ceremony anymore."

I lifted the lid from my soup and inhaled the delicious salty smell. My stomach growled and I realized I hadn't eaten since that morning when I'd had a bowl of cereal at the hotel. "Thank you for feeding me. It's very kind of you. But, please tell me before I die from curiosity." I looked him in the eye. "How do you know what I am?"

He picked his bowl up and took a sip of the steaming soup. His eyes met mine overtop of the ceramic, his eyebrows up high and his brows wrinkling. He set his bowl down. "I am surprised you would ask. As far as I know there is only one thing that could give away a Hanta in human form."

The surprise on his face made me shift in my seat uncomfortably. "I have been excessively sheltered," I said. It was the only explanation I had the ability to give.

"You have a smell like ozone. It's an odor I equate with lightning and thunder. Only creatures of the Æther have this scent, and Hantas have it the strongest. If I had not been saved by a Hanta one time in my life, I would not have known. The few people who smell you probably attribute it to a passing breath of fresh air. But I know better now." He lowered his voice and his eyes got a dreamy look. "It will be a beloved scent to me until the day they put me in the ground."

My skin prickled at the memory of Toshi whispering that I smelled like the air after a storm. My nose and eyes tingled and I blinked to clear them. I hadn't allowed myself to think about Toshi in years and suddenly he was as frequently in my mind as the sword I had come to retrieve. The pain that had dulled down to emotional scar-tissue over the years was once again acute and I steeled myself against the swell of grief that swept over me. "When was the last time you met a Hanta? Can you tell me what happened?"

Inaba nodded. "I have wanted the opportunity to tell someone my story for a long time. The Akuna Hanta is something that has faded completely into myth. No one would believe my story unless they'd been through something similar." He sat back and held out his arms. "Looking around, you may find it hard to believe that I was once a very wealthy and powerful man." He lowered his eyes. "I was. But no amount of wealth or power could possibly be worth what it cost me."

My gaze went up to the shelf where the two photographs sat. I nodded in their direction. "They were your wife and son?" It seemed safe enough to assume something had happened to separate Inaba from his family, for there were no signs of anyone else's existence in this small house aside from his.

He nodded. There was always the suggestion of a smile about his lips, but his brown eyes were heavy and sad. "I was already a member of the yakuza when I fell in love with Mihu. After we were married and she became pregnant with our son, she begged me to give up my yakuza life. But once you are a part of the organization, it is not so easy to get out. I understood my wife's fear, but we had a nice home and plenty of money, all because of the yakuza. I was not ready to leave. I knew I would one day. It is a violent and stressful life, but first I wanted to put aside enough money that we would never have to worry."

"Yakuza," I said, the word was unfamiliar to me. I broke it down into its three components and their Japanese meaning. "Eight, nine, and three?"

Inaba nodded. "That's right. The lowest score in the game of oichokabu, that is where the name originated. It literally means 'worthless.' The yakuza's roots are low, coming out of the Edo period some 350 years ago. At the time, they were nothing more than a bunch of misfits, peddlers, and gamblers. Now," he picked up his steaming cup of tea, "they are tens of thousands of members strong and operating in plain view of the police, who are too afraid to do anything about them."

I pictured a gang of street brawlers breaking windows and throwing homemade bombs into shops. Somehow, I thought that my imagination was more fueled by American movies I'd watched than reality. "So, they are like a gang? What do the yakuza do?"

"They are more than a gang." He laughed without any real humor. "And what *don't* they do is easier to answer. Where there is money, they have a hand in the pot—financial crimes, prostitution, drugs, corporate bribery. They are ruthless businessmen," he tilted his head, "and women, too, without any observation for the law. They follow their own laws. They are so much a part of the fabric of life in Japanese cities that they own or manipulate in some way all of the largest corporations in this country."

The blood drained from my face and I stared at my host. My life in a small village all those years ago had never been touched by corruption. The Japan Inaba was talking about was unfamiliar to me.

He put up a hand. "They are not always bad," he went on. "They are often the first to help in a crisis, provide aid after devastating natural disasters, and they even did much of the cleanup after the Fukishima disaster. They like to think they are the protectors of the weak." He shook his head. "I can speak so easily of them as something separate from me now, but truthfully, if Japan's government ever finds a way to bring them down, I should go down along with them. I had a hand in setting up the current regime. By the time my son Hiroki was born, my tattoos were already half complete, and I was losing my grip on reality."

"Your tattoos?" My eyes grazed his sleeves and his collar, looking for a trace of ink. I had seen photos of irezumi before, the Japanese full body tattoos, but never in person. "What do your tattoos have to do with anything?"

Inaba laughed. "Everything," he said, holding his arms out. "They have everything to do with it. And they have something to do with you, too."

My brows drew down in confusion and I wondered where this was going. "When you asked me to come here tonight, I came because I was under the impression that you would be able to help me locate the wakizashi. What do your tattoos have to do with that?"

"I did not mislead you, Akiko. Please," he put a hand out, "let me continue. You are the second Akuna Hanta I have encountered in my lifetime. There must be a reason for that, given that most people think you are a myth. Our meeting at the museum was not by chance. Let me help you."

I nodded. "Sorry to interrupt. Go on." I took three big swallows of the soup and it warmed my belly. I set the bowl down and waited.

"Traditionally, the yakuza choose the designs of tattoos because of the benefit they believe the symbol will bring them. Tigers for protection, koi for good luck, skulls to show respect for one's ancestors, and so on."

"Superstition." I nodded. Grandfather was superstitious, I had seen him salt our entrance and front steps before to dissuade beggars. My parents had been superstitious, too. Only Aimi seemed to be free from the chains of superstition. The irony in that almost made me laugh considering that she was a creature believed to belong to superstition.

Inaba leaned forward. "You could call it superstition, if you wanted. But I have since learned that it is an artfully executed deception."

"What do you mean? By who?"

"Do not make the mistake of thinking that those symbols do not hold power. I am living proof that they do. Rather, realize that the power that they have has been misconstrued. Carefully misrepresented over centuries to make men think one thing, when really the opposite is true. Their survival depends upon this deception holding fast, for if anyone knew what they were really doing when they tattooed them on their skin, no one would ever do so again."

"Whose survival?"

"The Oni."

My mind flashed back to paintings I had seen in my youth of a red-skinned ogre wielding a spiked club. I shivered.

"Ah, I can see from your face that you know what I am talking about." Inaba jabbed a finger toward me. "Am I also correct in guessing that you have not yet faced one of these entities? That your sheltered life has prevented you from doing your job?"

"No, I have never faced one." The idea of actually facing one of these creatures seemed an impossibility. If there were red-skinned flesh-eating ogres roaming the land, everyone would know about them. And if they were real, how was I, as a bird, supposed to kill one? The idea was absurd. There had to be more to it, and apparently this man knew what that *more* was. "What does this creature have to do with your tattoos?"

He sighed. "My arrogance had me choose the Oni for my irezumi. Most yakuza will allow the artist to choose the design, but I wanted an image that would strike fear into the hearts of my enemies and tell my yakuza brothers I was not to be challenged, so I made my own choice. Two Oni, one on my chest and the mirror image of him on my back. Irezumi are applied by hand with needles. It is a very slow, very painful process. Only a few yakuza manage to complete the entire body."

My eyes flashed to the fabric of his robe, so high up on his neckline. "And did you?" I couldn't help but want to see what was hiding under his clothing. Was it like the Oni images I remembered from my childhood?

"Yes. But no sooner had I completed the Oni on my torso when my thinking began to change. It was very subtle. There was no moment of possession that I can recall. It was a slow, insidious transition that I was unaware of at first. I no longer had thoughts of leaving the yakuza to retire. Instead I slid into thoughts of usurping the power of those above me, of setting traps for my brothers to remove them from my path and absorbing their income. The yakuza is close-knit, like a family. You swear allegiance to a symbolic father and to the community. There is nothing more important to the yakuza than the yakuza family. But, I no longer cared about these relationships, and even my wife and son came to mean less and less to me. I thrived on chaos, violence, and death. I began to crave the feeling of blood on my skin. It was not constant, you understand. Sometimes the Oni was there, ruling me from the inside. And sometimes its presence was not so apparent. It was in these moments that I became aware of what was happening. But the moment I thought of doing something about it, like praying, or arranging for an exorcism, it would rise up and swallow my intention with its own. I was no longer in control of myself."

"You believe this happened because of your tattoo?"

"At the time, no. It wasn't until after the Hanta saved me that I knew it was the tattoo that started it."

"I'm still not sure how that is possible. A tattoo is just ink."

He looked at me thoughtfully, searching for a better way to explain himself. "It's not the ink that matters, it's the image. Think of the Oni drawing like a brand or a logo. Someone or something, in this case a malicious spirit, owns the rights to that image. By tattooing its brand on my body in such a way, I was essentially giving it permission to access me, to own me."

A chill swept over my body and I shivered. "So how is it that it no longer has this access?"

"Two reasons." Inaba held up two fingers and I was reminded that he was missing the tip of his right pinky finger. I made a mental note to ask him about that next. "One—the Akuna Hanta rescued me. Two—I no longer have the tattoos."

My brows went up in surprise. Tattoos were permanent, and irezumi in particular covered the entire body. It would be impossible to remove them. "You had them removed? But how? I understand a small tattoo can be removed with a laser over many treatments, but—"

Inaba pulled his robe open, revealing his chest. His body from the collarbones down was a thick webbing of raised, scarred flesh. He looked like a burn victim. He had no nipples, for they too had been removed. "I had them flayed from my body."

Chapter Twelve

I leaned forward, my jaw growing slack as I took in the horror that was his skin. "You had the entire thing cut out? How did that not kill you?" My eyes roamed his chest. A network of deep crooked lines, like a topographical map or a jigsaw puzzle, crisscrossed everything I could see. Each piece of raised, scarred flesh in between the crevices was roughly the size of a man's palm.

"I did it in pieces, not all at once. There are lasers that will break up the ink and make them fade, but I needed all of the ink gone. I knew I wouldn't be free of the Oni otherwise. So I went to a specialist and she flayed it off, one piece at a time. When one patch had healed enough that the pain had gone away, I moved on to the next."

"Please tell me she used an anesthetic." I had started to sweat at the thought of a scalpel slowly cutting away pieces of hide, deep enough to take away the ink, while he sat still and allowed it. He must have been suffering horribly to choose the agony of being flayed over enduring his possession.

He shook his head. "It would have been pointless, really. Why block out the initial pain for a few moments when the regrowing of skin takes six months and is just as agonizing? Besides, I needed to feel it. For every piece of skin that was removed and replaced with scar tissue, I felt a little better, a little safer, a little more myself. Until finally," he gestured to his scarred torso, "it is nothing but a memory now. I took no photographs. The scars are more than enough to remind me of who I used to be."

"And the Akuna Hanta? How did he or she save you?"

Inaba closed his robe over his chest. "Earlier today I was hoping you could tell me that, but now I realize you can't." He scratched his chin thoughtfully. "My knowledge of your world is limited. I can only tell you my experience of it, what I can remember. The yakuza faction that I was a part of meets once a year on the island of Tai, just off the coast near Tottori."

I gasped. "I know the place! I grew up not far from there." Tai Island was visible from the clifftop where Toshi had first kissed me.

Inaba canted his head. "You are from the Tottori Prefecture?"

"Just outside. Furano was my home."

"I have never been to Furano, but Tottori is well known to me. I spent time there every year, always with the yakuza." Inaba paused. "When were you last there?"

"1923." The year I had lost my tamashī was a year I was not ever going to forget.

His smile melted away like butter in a hot oven and his face grew long with shock. "How long have you been in this sheltered circumstance?"

"Since then, and please do not ask any more questions about my circumstance. I won't be able to answer them."

Inaba's face took on a slightly gray cast and he frowned at me. "You were there long before Raiden's family bought the fortress. Long before Raiden was even a thought."

"Raiden?"

"The Kyoto yakuza family is led by a man named Raiden Yukimura. His family owns the fortress ruin on the island.

It's the perfect place to hide from prying eyes. There is no law there other than the law of the yakuza."

"What do they do there?"

"That part is not important to the story. The important part is that my state had been waxing worse and worse. I was still solidly in the yakuza fold since none of my crimes against them had yet been discovered. My presence was awaited there and I fully suspect that I was to be given more territory and power. My brutality had become legendary. But I was late for the meeting. A job that we needed to finish in Kyoto went badly and myself and the three other men were wounded. We missed our flight so we took a train to the coast and hired a private boat to take us to the island."

He took another sip of tea, and realized that his cup was empty. I picked up the teapot and poured for both of us. "Thank you," he said. "I was standing at the prow as we rode across the waves, when a large shadow passed overhead. Huge." He opened his arms and shook his head with wonder. "Like a dragon. I remember a loud crack of thunder and a flash of lightning. The smell of ozone was strong, so strong. I looked up, but I saw nothing amiss. No storm clouds." He laughed. "No dragons. I turned back to ask my companions if they had noticed, when the most peculiar feeling came over me. I can only describe it like my soul had snagged on something and was being stretched away from me like an elastic, right out the top of my head. The elastic snapped and I remember my neck recoiling, a sharp pain and then nothing."

I held my tea halfway to my lips, forgotten. "Nothing? That was it?"

"That was it," he shrugged. "I lost consciousness. I woke up on the floor of the boat sometime later with a flurry of voices around me. But the most wonderful thing was that I woke up clear-headed. I was thinking as clearly as I ever had before the tattoo. I was in charge of my own faculties once again." He chuckled and stroked his chin. "Then I had a problem. I knew that I had to get out of the yakuza. And that's when this happened." He held up his right hand, showing the missing section of pinkie finger. "It's yakuza tradition." He looked down at his mutilated pinkie. "If a member of the yakuza insults an elder, by way of apology, he offers up part of a digit. It is also done as a sacrifice when a member wants out. You have to cut it off yourself."

I closed my eyes as a wave of nausea passed through me. "That's barbaric," I said, shuddering as I imagined sending the blade of a knife down onto my own skin and bone. I opened my eyes. "Why?"

"It harkens back to the days of the samurai. A strong swordsman needed all of his fingers to wield a sword with skill. By removing knuckles, you become less effective at defending yourself, and more reliant on the group for survival. If you want to identify yakuza in public, it won't be by the tattoos, for they keep themselves covered. It'll be by what's missing from their hands." He held up his hand. "I am one of the lucky ones. The ones who make a lot of mistakes," he shook his head, "they end up missing a lot of fingers."

I took a sip of tea to moisten my throat, which had gone dry. "So, that time on the island fortress? You pled your case to leave the yakuza and offered up a," I swallowed down my nausea, "piece of your finger. And Raiden let you go free?"

"Well, at that time it was Raiden's father I was making the sacrifice to. But no, it wasn't as easy as that."

"Easy?" I almost laughed, and my eyes went to the hand holding the teacup. "There was something else you had to do? A toe, perhaps?"

Inaba laughed. "If only." He shook his head. "No. The yakuza do not like it when you leave. If you are lower down in the chain of command, you might be able to get away with leaving for the price of a fingertip. But I was a big fish. I was allowed to leave the island, but I had such unease about it. I knew that it wasn't over, and I was right."

He turned his head toward the shelf with the photographs on them.

I gasped. "Your family?"

"I should have known better." Inaba's eyes turned glassy and he lowered his gaze. For the first time since I had been in his company, he looked truly aged. His voice grew heavy, saturated with regret. "By the time I got home, Hiroki was gone. Mihu said they came for him in the middle of the night. They threw my wife in a closet, destroyed our home, and left with my son."

My jaw dropped. "Where did they take him?"

"It sounds horrible, and it was, but you have to know that Hiroki was eighteen by that time and had been raised with a yakuza father. He wanted into the organization, to follow his father's footsteps. I did not do a sufficient job in warning him of the realities of the yakuza life. He had romanticized the notion, and I had done nothing to disabuse him of it." He rubbed a palm down his face and tugged on his short beard. "I failed him. In my torpor and possession, I could not do what needed to be done while he was young."

"You're saying that even though they took him by force, Hiroki actually wanted to join them?"

He nodded. "His mother would never have allowed it. Their relationship was strained because of this. Eventually, he would have joined them. I am certain of it. There comes a point when a parent cannot direct a son's choices anymore. You've had your chance to parent your child and you don't get to do anything over." Inaba's eyes were filled with a heavy sadness.

"Could you not talk to him?"

His brown eyes found mine. "Do you think that I didn't try? My son made his choice. He no longer considers me a father. Turning my back on the yakuza has made me a coward in his eyes."

"He is still with them?"

"Far as I know, yes."

"And your wife?"

"She left me. She blamed me for Hiroki's choice, and she wasn't wrong. I can accept every accusation she would fling my way and would be guilty still of more than that."

The room lapsed into silence. I didn't know what to say. My own captivity, though it was everlasting, seemed to pale in comparison to the suffering and loss Inaba had endured.

Inaba's eyes brightened a fraction. "Not too long afterward, my son and wife were gone and I was a poor bachelor looking for honest work. I had submitted my application to a textile mill and it had not gone well." He held up his right hand again. "This betrays me wherever I go." He put his hand down. "I was sitting in a park not far from the mill. It was when the cherry trees were in blossom. I love that time of year. A young man with long black hair sat down beside me. I remember thinking he was the tallest and broadest man I had ever seen, with long powerful limbs. At first I thought he might be yakuza from another city, perhaps in Kyoto on business. I glanced at his hands, but he wasn't missing any fingers, and his sleeves were rolled up and there were no tattoos on his forearms. So I stayed on the bench and relaxed. Then a breeze came and blew the scent of this stranger toward me." Inaba shook his head and his eyes grew soft with affection. "That smell." He focused on me. "Your smell. It took me right back to the moment on the boat before I lost consciousness. I turned to look at him but he spoke first. He said, 'You are still in danger.'"

"He had been watching you?"

"I guess so. I thanked him for killing the Oni but he laughed and said, 'They cannot be killed. Or if they can, it is not my job to do it. It is my job to unseat them. You will make my job a lot more difficult if you remain marked the way you are.'"

"He was worried that you would become possessed again?"

"Yes. It was then that I realized how I had welcomed the attentions of the Oni. I began the flaying process immediately after that encounter."

"Did you ever see him again after that?"

Inaba shook his head. "No. There were times when the smell of ozone would come and go. I would look for him, but I never saw him again. My final flaying took place over twelve years ago now, and the first time I have smelled that scent since then was today, when you came into the museum. So you can understand now how I might feel like I owe your kind some sort of help. Whatever little I could offer."

A longing spiked through me to talk with this Hanta. "He never told you his name? Gave you a way to get in touch with him?"

Inaba gave a hearty belly laugh. "Why would he do that? You are creatures of the Æther, not doctors or dentists. If I could have him for dinner every week to have that scent around me and to ply him with questions, I would. He has more important things to do."

Yes, and so did I. I let Inaba's story sink in as I sipped the hot tea. This one conversation had done more to shed light on my purpose than any other I'd had, even the ones I'd had with Aimi so long ago. The desire to get the short sword and regain my freedom flared hot within me.

The Hanta who had helped Inaba had changed his whole life. It was too late to save his son and his marriage, but who knew what horrible things Inaba would have wreaked on Kyoto had the Oni been allowed to continue using him.

"Which brings us to you." Inaba's voice broke through my thoughts. "You wanted to see the swords that were on display in the museum?"

"Just one wakizashi. It has a blue handle and sheath, with a pattern of trees on it."

He tugged on his beard. "I have seen it. A beautiful piece of work. Why do you need to see it?"

"I don't need to see it." I hesitated before continuing, but Inaba had given me no reason not to trust him. "I need to steal it."

Inaba's eyes grew wide. "That seems a strange thing for Hanta to do."

"I can't explain, but it's very important. Without that sword—" The words froze up in my throat. My lips kept moving but no sound came out. The commands I was under silenced my voice.

Inaba shook his head. "I don't know what kind of trouble you are in, but I would advise you to find some other way to change your circumstance. A way that doesn't include that wakizashi. You may be immortal, but you can still be killed, am I right?"

"I think so," I said. My voice had returned but it was breathy.

"Then forget the wakizashi, please." His eyes turned pleading. "That sword belongs to a very dangerous collector. Taking it from him would be suicide."

"Whose is it?"

"Our earlier conversation will give you some idea of his notoriety. The sword belongs to Raiden Yukimura, the reigning yakuza father."

The small space grew heavy with silence. My heart thudded in the cavern of my chest. This was far worse than stealing an artifact from a museum. I could be killed in pursuit of it. I frowned, and another thought materialized.

I would rather die than face another hundred years as a slave.

"Raiden took the sword because he wanted it for the yakuza gathering on Tai Island. There are always ceremonial sword fights during these events. The yakuza enjoy sparring with one another, Raiden above all. He is impulsive and subject to changes in mood. He might have been feeling generous when he agreed to loan it to the museum, but apparently he changed his mind and decided he wanted it back. The museum would not dare protest. I warned the supervisor that putting the sword in their promotional materials was courting disappointment."

A horrifying thought came to mind. "Were you there when Raiden came to take it from the museum?"

"I was. But don't be concerned, I am of no consequence to Raiden anymore. He has my son, he destroyed my marriage. I am subdued. He didn't even look at me."

I chewed my lip, visualizing the fortress on the distant island. I never thought I would see the places of my childhood ever again. Instead, it seemed I was destined to return, for the sake of my freedom.

"Have I dissuaded you?" came Inaba's voice, quiet and hopeful.

Bring me this wakizashi and I will give you your freedom.

"No," I said.

Inaba frowned and then leaned forward. "Is getting this wakizashi important enough to risk your life for it?"

"Yes," I said stoutly. "This task is the only thing that matters right now."

Inaba sighed. "I hope that your Hanta abilities can provide you with enough stealth and wits to carry out such a suicide mission. It might not be difficult to find a way in, for you are a beautiful young woman. Beautiful women are a fixture at yakuza events. The difficulty lies in getting out. Especially in possession of one of Raiden's prized artifacts." Inaba's gaze held mine and the warning in it brought cold into my bones. "You will need more than luck to succeed. That fortress will be crawling with yakuza."

Chapter Thirteen

The train to Tottori wound swiftly and smoothly through the scenic mountain ranges of the Chugoku region. City and town went by in a blur, all nestled in vibrant green trees, along valley floors and staggered along the mountainsides. Excitement buzzed in my stomach like bees as I got closer and closer to my old home. The Tottori prefecture was the least populous region in Japan even to the present day. Rich with natural parks, famous for waterfowl and the largest sand dunes in the country, the Chugoku region was nearly intoxicating in its beauty.

I stepped off the train at dusk, inhaling the air of my childhood. It had the same sweet and salty tang, the same cloying humidity. Tears pricked my eyes and I closed them. The lined faces of my parents flashed in my memory, my mother's soft brown eyes, my father's high strong cheekbones. Toshi's image materialized, still young and beautiful. Had he had a good life? Had he married Aimi after I disappeared? If he had, had she been good to him? The knife of remorse and anger at what had been stolen from me sliced through my heart and forced me to take a seat on a bench outside the train station. Bitterness filled my mouth at the thought of Aimi's betrayal. Where was she now?

My legs trembled as I left the train station for the main street and the hotel room I had booked from Kyoto. Later, once the wakizashi was in my possession and my task was finished, I would go to the Susumu family grave. If I didn't die before then.

My room was spare but clean, with a single bed and a tiny bathroom. I locked the door and inspected my meager surroundings, looking for the most important feature of the room—the safe. I had spent the better part of a morning calling hotels to confirm that each room had a safe. It took over a dozen calls to find one with a safe large enough for a short sword.

I stripped off my clothes and underwear, folded them and put them in a drawer. I put my purse into the safe along with my cell phone, ID, and wallet. I took my hair out of its clip and shook it out. I took my black silk robe, folded it into a collar and knotted it around my throat.

I opened the single window and the shutters. Fresh evening air blew over my naked form. I took a deep breath, visualizing Tai Island. I didn't need a map to know where I was going. For many years I had thought of Tai Island as my island. I lifted my arms and let the feeling of phasing sweep over me as I transformed into a strix, a small owl. I hopped up on the windowsill, scrabbling on the smooth wood with my black talons, my wings out for balance. I'd have to leave the window open because I couldn't shut it in this form.

Getting the edge of the sill under my claws for leverage, I opened my wings fully and took off silently into the evening.

The world looked completely different through my owl eyes. The form I had chosen was equipped with silent wings and binocular vision, especially powerful at night. I could hear a mouse stepping on a twig over eighty feet away. My strix face was shaped like a satellite dish, capturing everything going on in front of me.

I headed straight for the ocean and then south along the coast, riding the air currents coming off the water. The sounds of rodents, other birds, and even insects became the backdrop as I focused in on human noises—voices carrying over the water, the sound of a chain rattling along a wooden dock, and the stacking of plastic bins as fishermen cleaned up a boathouse. The scent of smoke from their cigarettes didn't bother me, since I had no sense of smell, but for a brief moment it assaulted my lungs. I gave a small owl cough and flew higher.

Tai Island soon appeared as a jagged shape on the horizon. I caught an updraft as I tilted away from land and flew across the water. I could take the shape of a bird, but I was unencumbered by a bird's instinct; instead my mind toiled over the task ahead of me. I had no real ability to plan my break-in and break-out until I knew what I was dealing with. As long as I was in winged form, I was safe. The danger would come when I had to become human again.

The island zoomed by underneath me. It was a sharp contrast of rocks and trees, bare slabs of gray rock dotted with green moss. The sounds of voices and boat engines became distinct. The Tai Island fortress appeared as I crested a bluff. If I had been in human form, my jaw might have dropped. The fortress was enormous and striking. Half built upon a rocky promontory jutting out into the sea, the outer walls seemed to rise up into the sky forever. Surrounded by a rectangular courtyard stood the heart of the fortress and the most spectacular tiered structure. The corners of each roof winged up slightly in classic pagoda style. Built by the Imperial Japanese Army, behind the outer walls there would lay a labyrinth of interconnected underground passages and trenches connecting every above ground emplacement and every below ground bunker.

Some buildings and sections of wall were crumbling and overgrown with vines and moss. Only half of the fortress was lit, the half closest to the ocean and the center fort. Three of the six floors of the interior castle were illuminated.

I winged over the courtyard and settled in the branches of a tree. Sitting still, with only my head rotating on its axis, I took in the full view of the courtyard, the open gate leading to a dock, and the front steps of the castle. The ground was steep and uneven, leading down to the sea. At the lowest point was an open gate where new arrivals would enter. The sound of a boat could be heard through the open gate and voices on the other side of it.

A new wave of yakuza poured in through the gate. Men in simple clothing and demure postures appeared from the castle and descended the steep crumbling steps to meet the arrivals. Luggage, both square and strangely-shaped, was ferried into smaller buildings. It was easy to separate the servants from the masters during all this activity.

Men and women, dressed mostly in business attire, strolled the overgrown and unmanicured gardens in the courtyard. They smoked and talked in small groups. My owl eyes easily picked out many hands with missing fingers.

As a bird, my sense of time was tied to the movement of the sun and moon, and the changing light throughout the day. It was easy for me to tell how the hours were passing within any one day, but pile day upon day and I easily lost track of time. I sat in that tree until the sky grew black and the human shapes all drifted inside the castle. More lights flickered on and the sound of talk seeping from the windows thickened.

I flew to the eaves of the first-floor roof and landed, changing into a pigeon. I hopped along the eaves, soundless, my little head darting and listening. I found an open window and dropped onto the sill, peeking inside.

The interior of this room was dark and heavy with wooden beams and timbers. People sat in small groups, talking. A wall to the rear of the room slid sideways and a woman in full geisha dress entered, carrying a tray of drinks. She floated through the room like a ghost, as though simply standing on an invisible conveyer belt

The sound of women's voices talking softly behind me had me flitting back up the eaves and taking the shape of the strix again. At least a dozen women, all petite, slender, and attractive, were being escorted from the gate to a building across the courtyard, separate from the castle fortress. I watched them walk, heads tilted slightly down, glossy black hair reflecting the moonlight, floating along on tiny steps. More geisha, I guessed.

Women's voices directed my attention back to the gate, these ones louder, and with more laughter. Half a dozen women followed the first group, but these without the mincing steps. All of them were blondes. They went to yet another building.

I watched as the last of the geisha disappeared into a small castle structure of their own, followed by a couple of older-looking women. My opportunity had presented itself.

At the sound of another boat engine, I flew over the court-yard and past the outer wall. There, I perched in a tree where I could see the dock. The lights of two more motor boats were drawing close to the dock where men stood waiting to help unload the boats.

I watched as another dozen women were helped onto the dock. The same older lady I had seen leading the first batch of girls appeared from the fortress entrance and picked her way down the dark steps and to the trees. I could see easily that she was unsure of her footing from the lack of light. The steps were uneven, and probably slick with moisture. She wore a black suit jacket and slacks and had a small clipboard in her hand and a pen between her teeth.

She finally made it to the water's edge, stepped up to the dock, and clapped her hands like she was herding schoolchildren, not grown women. The ladies gathered close and I could hear the madam taking a kind of roll call. All of the women carried purses, but only some of the women were carrying larger bags. Costumes, I presumed.

Satisfied that her girls were accounted for, the madam led them off the dock and up the stone steps.

Two possibilities raced through my mind. I could change now in the privacy of the bushes and trail behind the last girl, hoping that no one noticed in the dark, or find a way inside the fortress as a bird and change then. I didn't know what awaited me once I was inside, so this opportunity seemed as good as any.

I flew into the bushes near the walkway, dumped my black silk onto the earth, and phased. Twigs poked and scratched me everywhere as I scrambled to undo the knot in my robe. I pulled on my thin covering and the silk slippers and crawled closer to the stairs where I could see feet taking the steps up and heard the chatter of multiple female voices. My heart hammered in my chest so hard I felt breathless. As the last pair of legs passed, I glanced at the boat dock and saw the dock men chatting with the drivers and paying no attention. Quick as I dared, I slipped out from the bushes and silently fell in line behind the last girl. Fighting to keep control of my breathing, I followed the crew, feeling like any moment a hand was going to clamp down on my shoulder and single me out. But the madam was far ahead, and the girls were so busy chattering that no one seemed to notice the small girl in the black silk robe and slippers.

Heart pounding, I marched through the courtyard and up the steps of one of the fortress buildings.

Chapter Fourteen

"We are falling behind schedule," snapped the madam, clapping her hands sharply together. For a moment, I was reminded of my mother, clapping her hands to move Aimi and me along whenever we dawdled. I found myself ushered down a hallway and into a room full of steam and lined with showerheads. The tile floors tilted toward a drain and soapy water swirled and gurgled as it disappeared into the floor. Robes were hung on pegs just inside the door, and reluctantly, I took off my black silk and hung it up. My body was immediately damp.

Pale bodies slick with soap and water stood under every showerhead, scrubbing and shampooing. There was some nervous laughter and conversation in low voices. The tension in the room was even thicker than the steam.

"There," the woman said, hooking a hand under my elbow and pointing to a showerhead which had just become free. The girl who had turned off the water was wrapping herself in a cotton towel. She handed me a slimy bar of soap as we passed.

"Have you done this before?" I asked the girl beside me, whose head was white with suds.

She squinted at me with one eye before closing it again and tilting her head back under the spray to rinse. "Nervous?"

"A little," I replied. In fact my knees felt weak with fear.

"You're here with me, so you're not a trained maiko, or a geisha. Just mimic them as best you can and you should be fine. Don't say or do anything stupid, and try to go for the ones that smile and laugh a lot."

"Mimic the geisha? Which ones are the geisha?" I craned my neck at the women around me.

"They're getting ready in another room. They keep their costumes locked up. Full geisha dress and jewelry is worth well over three million yen." She lowered her voice, and added, "And they don't trust anyone here."

I blinked at her. "And what are we?"

She flipped off the water and grabbed a towel from an overhead rack. I did the same.

"We're the pretenders," she said, surprised. "Your house didn't prepare you very well, did they. Where do you come from?" She grabbed a second towel, blotted her face, and wrapped up her hair.

"Oh, uh, Kyoto." I dried my skin off.

"Me too. Which house?" She headed for the door.

My stomach was spiraling downhill fast, along with the situation. What if this girl found out I was an imposter? I said the first vague thing I could think of. "It's a house in Yamashina Ward."

She frowned. "I didn't know there was a house in that area." She grabbed a cloth bag from a peg by the door and I snagged my black silk and followed her out into the cool dark hallway.

She introduced herself as Chiyoko and I gave my name as Yokana.

"Not enough trained geisha, and no real maiko at all say yes to these events. So they hire us to bolster the numbers," she said under her breath as we wandered along the cold stone floor. "They dress us similar to geisha but with enough differences that the men can tell us apart. That way if we slip up, they are more forgiving."

"Slip up?" I asked as my teeth began to clack from the cold.

She pushed her way into another room. A space heater stood in the center and I sighed with pleasure as the heat washed over my freezing and wet skin.

"Yes, with the geisha way," she said. "Why don't you take thc place beside mine? It's free. I know how you feel. It was my first year oncc too. It's a little nerve-wracking, but you'll be okay."

Right.

I froze when I saw the vanity lights and mirrors lining the wall and realized that every girl here was applying makeup from a personal makeup bag.

"Think they'll notice if I don't wear any makeup?" I asked with a laugh.

She gave an authentic belly-laugh until her eyes skimmed me and realized I actually didn't have a makeup bag. She stopped laughing and her eyes grew wide. "You're not joking, are you?"

I shook my head and bit my lip, giving her my best 'please help me' expression. "I was told the makeup would be provided," I whispered.

She let out a long breath. "Your house sisters must hate you." She put a hand on my forearm and her eyes darted about the room before settling on me again. "They've played a terrible joke on you, and shame on them for it. If Madam Kameyo knew, you would be taken aside and punished."

I let my eyes grow round with fear. Little did this girl know that I was up against someone a lot more terrifying than Madam Kameyo.

"Don't worry," she said quickly. "I'll help you." She shifted her makeup bag over so it sat between us. "We can help each other, in fact. My partner from last year didn't come this year. Something happened to her last time that must have frightened her." She unscrewed the lid from a pot of white paste and picked up a brush with wide flat bristles. She fished in the bag and pulled out a fat hair clip. "Here, tie your hair back."

"Something frightened her? Like what?" I asked as I twisted my wet locks up and clipped them to the top of my head.

Chiyoko took my chin in her fingers and lifted my face to the light. "I'm sure you can guess," she said. "What do you think happens at an event where we are not allowed to say 'no'?" She said this so matter-of-factly that I had to wonder for a second if I had heard her correctly. "Well," she rolled her eyes. "You are allowed to say no," she added, "but they *advise against it.*" She said it with emphasis gave me a look full of meaning. "Not something I would really want to test," she said under her breath. She dipped the brush in the paste and began to paint my cheeks with the cool mixture.

My fingers became ice-cold. I hoped she wasn't talking about what I thought she was talking about. "Say no to... a game of poker?" I raised an eyebrow. "Beer? Making papier-mâché masks?"

She bit back a smile. "Nice to see you have a sense of humor about it." She frowned and paused in applying my make-up. "I'm sorry your sisters didn't prepare you better. It's not funny to play with someone's career like that."

I made an appropriately angry face. "Yes, I will have to talk to them when I get back."

"Shhh," she shushed me as she painted under my nose, across my lips and down my chin. "Be still or I will make a mess." She dipped the brush again and painted my forehead, earlobes, cheekbones and jaw. The brush strokes tickled under my chin and down my neck. "Turn please." Chiyoko's fingers gripped my shoulders and I turned around so my back was to the lights. "Collar," she said.

Somewhere in the deepest recesses of my memory I recalled some village girls in Furano whispering about how the geisha leave two stripes of clean, makeup-free skin down the back of their neck. I pulled my robe down off my shoulders and held it closed in front of my chest.

Chiyoko's fingers tilted my head forward. The brush strokes down the back of my neck and across my upper back made me shiver.

"I know," Chiyoko said. "This part always gives me goose-bumps, too." The brush strokes slowed down as she applied the white paste, leaving two inverted triangles down either side of the back of my neck. "Okay, face me again."

I turned back to Chiyoko's critical gaze as she inspected her work. "What do you think? Good enough?"

I looked at myself in the mirror and gave a start. The ghost staring back at me looked nothing like me. Even my lips and eyebrows were completely white. My usually light golden eyes looked almost black peering out from the pale geisha mask my face had become.

"Looks good," I said, hoarsely. I cleared my throat and fought the urge to scratch an itch on my cheek.

She nodded and handed me the pot and the brush. "Sorry, I only have one brush," she said shrugging. "Beggars can't be choosers." She closed her eyes and tilted her face up to the light for me.

"It's nice of you to share." I dipped the brush in the makeup. As I painted Chiyoko's face in the same way she'd done mine, I found myself thinking that in another time, another place, another circumstance, Chiyoko and I might have been friends.

Chiyoko became a porcelain doll in front of my eyes. The paint erased all natural skin color and covered every freckle, mole, and scar.

"So, is this event always on Tai Island?" I asked.

Without opening her eyes, Chiyoko made a sound of affirmation. "For as long as I've been coming, anyway," she mumbled through stiff lips, trying not to move.

"I heard," I said casually, "that Mr. Yukimura has quite a collection of samurai artifacts on display here. Do you remember seeing anything like that here last year?" I dipped and painted, dipped and painted, across her jaw, down her neck to her collarbones.

"Turn?" she asked, eyes still closed. "Feels like you're done the front."

"Yes."

She turned her back to me and tilted her face forward. "There were some nice decorations in the great room last year. I don't know if they were actual artifacts or just replicas, but knowing Mr. Yukimura, I wouldn't doubt their authenticity. He has a reputation for being a generous patron to the museums in Kyoto."

"Oh, really? That's nice of him." I was proud of myself for keeping a straight face. "Is the great room where the party is?"

"Yes, but there are a lot of other rooms used for more private parties and things." She frowned. "At least I would guess that's what they're for. Don't really know. I've never seen anything aside from the great room and a few of the suites upstairs. The place is a maze, and Madam Kameyo doesn't like it if we wander for no reason."

"Right." My skin prickled at the thought of what Chiyoko would have been doing with the yakuza in those upstairs suites. "But if I got one of them to show me around? Just a little tour for interest's sake?"

Chiyoko shrugged. "If you're with one of them, you can go anywhere." She cocked her head to look at me out the corner of her eye. "You're really curious about this place?"

"I love history," I said. "Straighten please."

She put her face forward, straightening her neck for me. "Just make sure you keep the conversation about them and not about you," she added. "These men love to have a woman think they're fascinating and that they know everything."

This seemed like excellent advice. "Thanks for that," I said, and meant it. I painted the back of her neck and upper back, leaving her skin blank and making the smooth lines as best I could.

"The irony is that half of these girls are university students. Med students and law students. Brilliant women playing simpletons for the night." For the first time since I'd met her, I heard bitterness creep into her tone. "Some of them will get tangled up in relationships with men here."

"I can only imagine," I said, putting the finishing touches on her makeup. "Okay, I think you're good."

Chiyoko turned to me and put a hand on my forearm. She held my gaze. "Don't get involved," she warned.

My heart melted at the sincerity for my well-being in her eyes. "Don't worry, Chiyoko. That won't happen."

"And, don't forget. They made you sign a non-disclosure agreement for a reason. When you leave this place, you don't talk about anything you saw or heard."

"Of course," I said. They had these girls sign NDAs? A thousand imaginary spiders walked across my skin. What went on in this place?

Chiyoko squeezed my arm and nodded. She looked in the mirror to examine her makeup. She turned her face this way and that. She pulled out a small hand-mirror and used it to look at the back of her neck in the big mirror. "Good job," she said. "At least your sisters are teaching you to apply makeup correctly."

I almost laughed. Makeup had never been my strong suit. My collection was limited to an old dried-out tube of mascara, clear lip gloss, and three pots of colored glitter that Saxony had given me as a gift for a birthday a few years ago. I had been turning 'fifteen' and Saxony hadn't known me well enough to realize that I wouldn't use glitter unless at gunpoint. With Saxony, it really was the thought that counted.

Chiyoko applied my brow and eye makeup, painting the outer corners of my eyes with bright pink. She chattered quietly about the sisters back at her house, how she had an allergic reaction to the first white makeup she tried, and how in the old days, there was lead in the makeup which made the geisha sick.

The soft brush strokes across my eyes and the murmuring sweetness of her voice worked to calm my nerves. The other girls applying makeup and doing their hair around us faded into the background and I could almost convince myself that we were not a bunch of women preparing to entertain criminals, but just young ladies bonding over makeup and hair talk. A stab of longing for my friends passed through me and I wondered what they were up to. Jealousy for the safety of a normal life was the aftertaste.

Chiyoko put the finishing touches on my bottom lip with red paint and leaned back to admire her handiwork. "When your hair is done, you won't look any different than a real Maiko," she said.

I held out my hand for the makeup but she shook her head. "I'll do my own eyes—it's my favorite part and no one else ever gets it right. No offense."

"None taken," I said with relief. I took my damp hair down and frowned. If Chiyoko expected me to do my own hair in a geisha style, or worse—hers, then she was going to be terribly disappointed.

Chiyoko eyed me. "Go see Madam Kameyo. We get wigs as part of our costumes."

"Oh." I spied the fierce-looking woman by the door speaking to a young woman in glasses. Madam Kameyo had her finger in the girl's face and the girl was nodding, her eyes downcast. I gulped and steeled my nerves. I wandered over and stood there quietly until the two were done talking and the young woman left the room.

Madam Kameyo spied me. "Come," she said, waving me closer with a sharp hand movement. She grasped my shoulders. "Face," she barked.

I tilted my face up so she could see it. She inspected, making a grunt of approval. "Go to the next room. Miyoko will give you the rest. Tell her I said the chrysanthemum. Go."

I stepped out into the cool hallway and went to the next door. I raised my knuckles to rap but the door opened and a tall woman dressed from head to toe like a geisha came out. She walked by me, gliding like a ghost. I couldn't help but watch her slide away, silent but for the soft rustle of fabric, her hips swaying under the belt cinching in her waist.

"Well, don't stand there gaping, come in," said a voice.

I stepped into a small space with boxes and bags everywhere. A full length mirror stood in front of a small platform. The woman in the glasses from earlier stood folding up fabric and glanced at me when I came in. Another older woman with enormous glasses tilted her head back to peer at me, her eyes as enormous as an owl's.

"You must be Miyoko," I said, a tremor in my voice. I cleared my throat. "Madam Kameyo said the chrysanthemum."

"What? Speak up, girl," barked the woman in glasses.

"She said the chrysanthemum," I repeated, louder and more confident this time.

Miyoko snorted and put her hands on her hips. "Did she?" She eyed my form from head to toe. "Well, she has no idea what I have in my inventory." She bent and rifled through a nearby box, muttering to herself. She pulled out a clear plastic bag with blue fabric inside. She pulled it out and tore the bag open. "I say the blue with the cranes will suit you best." She pulled out a robe of bright robin's egg blue and shook it open. She threw it at the other girl and went back to her rummaging.

The other girl waved me over and I stood in front of the mirror. What followed was a lot of turning and lifting my arms as the younger woman swathed me in meters and meters of fabric. My hair was spiraled up and shoved under a tight net cap. An elaborate black wig was placed over the cap and fasted with tiny clips. By the time she was tying the thick belt around my waist, I had begun to sweat.

The last thing to be sorted were the shoes. White socks specially made with a space between my big toe and second toe encased my feet. I stared at the five-inch tall flipflops the young woman shoved in front of my feet. I slipped a foot in, sliding the thong into place. I stepped up onto the first one and then slid my other foot home.

I looked at myself in the mirror and stared for a full minute. Staring back was a geisha who could have stepped out from an ancient tapestry. If I didn't move or blink, I looked like a perfect doll. The red paint on my bottom lip gave me a supernatural pout, and the pink makeup on my eyes reminded me of cherry blossoms. The wig on my head could easily have been mistaken for my own hair. It curved wildly out in upside down cups which covered my ears and arched up high over the crown of my head. A silver clip with dangling blue beads hung down to my cheekbone and swung around as I moved my head.

"How will they know I'm not a real geisha?" I said, my voice an octave higher than normal.

Miyoko rolled her eyes and shook her head. "I swear, the more beautiful they are the more empty their brains," she muttered. She turned away and folded up a discarded robe.

The woman in the black glasses leaned close and said quietly: "No obi belt. Don't mind her. She forgets sometimes that most of the girls here are untrained."

"Do we get a...a crash course?" I asked.

"Sorry," the young woman shook her head and stood up. "You'll have to ask one of the other girls. If you didn't think you could do a convincing job, you shouldn't have signed the contract." She picked up a bunch of discarded plastic bags and then stopped, eyeing what must have been terror on my face. "You look great though," she said cheerfully.

Chapter Fifteen

As soon as she was finished dressing me, Miyoko told me I was free to go to the castle and join the party already underway. Instead, I went back to the dressing room to find Chiyoko. Only a few girls remained, putting the final touches on their makeup. Chiyoko wasn't there. I thought she must have headed to the party and turned to leave. I opened the door just as she was coming in.

"Wow," she said. "You look amazing." She scanned me from wig to platform shoes. "You clean up well."

"So do you," I smiled.

Chiyoko was dressed in a pink kimono with a dense pattern of bamboo leaves reaching up from the hem. A green belt cinched her in at the waist and a wig similar to mine covered her real hair.

"Ready?" she asked.

"As I'll ever be," I said.

Chiyoko gestured to a couple of other girls in the room. "Toshiko, Yuko, are you ready to come down?"

"A few more minutes," waved the one in the bright green kimono. "You go ahead."

Chiyoko nodded and hooked a hand under my elbow. We made our way across the courtyard together to the castle.

"Any last minute tips?" I said, my hands and feet clammy from nerves.

"Try not to let your head bob up and down when you walk, take smaller steps," she lowered her voice as we passed two men standing on a patch of grass and smoking cigarettes. They nodded to us and Chiyoko lowered her eyes and her chin toward them. I did my best to mimic her.

I shortened up my steps and tried to make my gait smooth. "Like this?"

"Better," she said. "Don't make any fast movements. Everything should be slow and graceful. When you have to open a door, always go to your knees first. Slide the door open, get up, go through, kneel again, and slide the door closed."

I closed my eyes, committing her words to memory. "Okay, what else?"

"Always serve them first. Whatever they're drinking, make sure their glass is always full and don't take a drink of anything until they've had a sip first. Don't be loud, no matter how much they make you drink."

"Right." I hadn't thought about that. Of course there was going to be alcohol here, and of course I was going to have to drink. I had never had more than a few glasses of hot sake in my life. At less than a hundred pounds and with no tolerance whatsoever, having my judgement clouded by alcohol was a very real danger.

"If the conversation stalls, suggest a drinking game," Chiyoko said. "They love drinking games."

"Great." What was a drinking game?

We ascended the stone steps to the fortress and nodded to more men standing outside and chatting under the torches. Chiyoko lowered her voice even more. "Laugh at their jokes, but not too loud. Make them feel like you're falling in love with them. After dinner, I can guarantee you that a beautiful girl like you will be asked to go upstairs."

I swallowed hard. I wouldn't let it get that far.

She squeezed my arm. "I do not recommend that you say 'no.' They say you have a choice, obviously, but it's the nature of this job to be a trap. If you do a good enough job making them feel like big men, they will want to take you to bed. If you say no, you risk insulting them." Her voice went right down to a whisper. "And that is not something I recommend you do in this company."

By the time we glided through the dark, expansive foyer of the castle, I was sweating like I'd just sprinted a mile. My heart was thudding so loudly I could hear it echoing off my wig and back into my eardrums. My hands were clammy and I wanted to scratch all the makeup off my face and cut the restrictive kimono off my body with the biggest pair of shears I could find. Regret soured in my mouth. What had I done? I should have found a way to explore the castle as a bird. Why had I chosen to disguise myself?

"Are you okay?" Chiyoko faced me just outside of a closed sliding door. The room on the other side of the door was filled with the sound of voices, traditional Japanese music, and cutlery and clinking glasses. The smells of fried fish, rice, and cooked vegetables filled the foyer.

"Yes," I said through numb lips.

"You'll be fine," she said, her white face seeming expressionless and ghostly in the gloom of the foyer.

She knelt at the door and I knelt behind her. She slid the door open and the noise of the party hit me in the chest. There was no turning back now. Chiyoko got up gracefully and passed through the open door. I followed her and mimicked her every move as she turned to face the door, knelt, and closed it.

Inside the door were four steps leading down to a large space filled with clusters of low tables. Women dressed like maiko glided about carrying trays of food and drinks, and they were distinguishable by the red paint on only their bottom lips. Both geisha, and Caucasian women in gorgeous dresses and high heels, mingled with men dressed in beautifully tailored suits. Chains glinted at the men's necks, and thick rings brought attention to meaty fingers with portions missing from the knuckles.

At the end of the room, opposite the bar, three geisha danced gracefully to the music of the junanagen and koto, traditional Japanese instruments which were played by two more geisha. Each woman was resplendent in a brightly colored costume and obi-belt.

A few eyes assessed us from the din, but most people didn't notice the two new girls who had entered. I was painfully self-aware of the awkwardness of entering a party where I knew no one. Saxony would be able to navigate something like this like a pro, but I was a textbook introvert.

I followed Chiyoko to the bar at the back of the room, trying to look like I belonged there. A couple of men stood leaning against the bar and drinking beer. They straightened as we approached.

"Hideo," said Chiyoko, smiling and inclining her head. I almost gaped at her. Her voice had transformed. It dripped honey. "How lovely to see you again."

"The fragrant lily returns," said the taller man in the navy suit jacket. A long chain with thick links disappeared under his purple button-down shirt. He took Chiyoko's hand and kissed it. His eyes fell on me. "Who is your beautiful friend?"

"This is Yokana." Chiyoko put a hand on my shoulder. "This is her first year at Tai Island."

I smiled and dipped my chin. "A pleasure to meet you, Hideo."

Hideo introduced his friend as Ryota. Ryota was older, shorter, and broader than his friend. He didn't say anything when introduced, just dropped his chin with a jerk. His calculating eyes examined my face and hair.

"Have you eaten?" Chiyoko asked.

"No, in fact. A table has just come free. Would you like to join us?" Hideo asked.

"We would like nothing more," Chiyoko said.

The men led the way to a small square table near an open window.

I followed Chiyoko's lead in everything, seating myself the same way she did, and holding my hands in my lap.

Ryota had still said nothing and when Chiyoko fell into conversation with Hideo, I leaned forward and said the only thing that came to my mind. "Have you been here before, Ryota?"

"Many times." His voice was rough, like he had a sore throat. "This is our biggest yearly event, but there are many smaller meetings throughout the year..."

I listened politely as Ryota talked, but my mind was racing for a way to bring the conversation around to the fortress and where I might find the swords. Once he got talking, he didn't shut up, and I was grateful for not having to say much aside from polite expressions of interest.

Steaming food appeared before us, as well as drinks, and the four of us could have looked like old friends from the outside. I was too riddled with anxiety to have any appetite, but at urging from Ryota I took small bites. Everything smelled delicious, but it tasted like sawdust in my mouth. My sake cup was never empty and I followed

Chiyoko's lead by taking very small but frequent sips. Every movement she made was feminine and delicate. I doubted I looked so natural playing the part of a geisha, but after a few cups of hot sake, I didn't care. My thinking grew a little fuzzy around the edges and as another cup was filled in front of me, I frowned. I was letting too much time go by. I had to get out of here.

Emboldened by the alcohol, I put a palm on Ryota's hand. "I have heard there are some wonderful samurai artifacts here in the fortress. Have you seen them?"

Ryota's cheeks were tinged with pink, but his eyes were clear as he smiled at me. "There are, and I have. Would you like to see them?"

I didn't have to fake the delight on my face. I put my palms together. "I would love to. Would you show me?"

"Of course. Why don't we go now?" Ryota said, putting down his glass of beer. He leaned in conspiratorially. "That way we'll have them to ourselves."

My smile wavered at the idea of being alone with Ryota, but I wasn't about to pass up the chance. "All right."

Ryota excused us and Chiyoko's eyes found mine as I stood. I gave her a smile to reassure her that I was okay.

"See you later," she said.

"Enjoy," I responded. Ryota tucked my hand into the crook of his elbow and led me from the great room and into the foyer. We crossed the foyer and went up wide wooden stairs to a second level. The temperature was cooler up here, and the only source of light came from a few dim sconces on the wooden walls.

"Raiden is quite a collector," Ryota said as we walked down a narrow hallway, our footsteps echoing. He gripped my cold hand in his warm one.

"So I've heard," I said.

He looked down at me. "Are you cold?"

"No, I'm fine, thank you," I said.

Ryota paused outside a sliding door and glanced around as though he wasn't sure if we were supposed to be here. He slid the door back and stood aside to let me enter first.

The room was an office. A large wooden desk dominated the space, with library shelves including cubby-holes filled with scrolls behind it. Two windows allowed moonlight into the room, but Ryota reached for a switch and an overhead chandelier dusted everything in a dim yellow glow.

"Wow," I said, stepping into the space, my eyes immediately flying around the room in search of my sword.

Two full suits of samurai armor on dummies stood in the corners behind the desk, and a rack on the desk carried two katanas and one wakizashi. Aside from these there were no other weapons in the room that I could see. My heart dropped when I stepped closer and realized that the short sword was not the one Daichi wanted. It was sheathed in dark brown leather.

"Aren't they beautiful," Ryota said, staring at one of the samurai helmets.

"They are," I agreed, but inside my mind was racing. There were no cupboards or closets in the small room, and while it was filled with other artifacts, maps, and artwork, strange metal devices I couldn't identify—my wakizashi was not here.

Ryota and I turned when a deep voice said, "I see we are not the first to have this idea."

We turned to see another yakuza man with a drop-dead gorgeous blond woman in a spectacular sparkling dress. A deep neckline showed off enormous pale breasts and the yellow light made the woman's hair look like spun gold. In sparkly black stilettos, she towered over her partner. The hem of her dress ended at mid-thigh and her long slender legs glimmered with shimmery moisturizer. She looked like she'd just walked off the Miss Universe stage.

"Oh, excuse us," she said in near-perfect Japanese. She hooked an arm under her partner's arm and turning toward the door as though to leave us alone. "I was just curious about the armor. We'll come back later."

The moment I saw the look on Ryota's face, that said he was in the presence of a goddess, my heart felt full of gratitude for her. "No, please," I said. "Come in, come in. We would be happy for your company." My voice radiated warmth and welcome, and even I had to admit, it sounded nothing like me.

"Yes, indeed," said Ryota, his eyes glued to the blonde's bountiful chest. "Join us."

The couple hesitated, shared a look, and then came back inside the office.

"Isn't the armor spectacular," I said. "You must see the leather work; it's breathtaking."

"Oh yes?" the woman said, brightening. She and her partner came to join Ryota and me standing near the dummy.

"Oh, you are right," she breathed. "Look at this detail," she said to the man with her, who made a sound of admiration.

I caught a look at Ryota's facc and was satisfied to see that he was still staring at the statuesque woman, his jaw slightly slack.

The blonde and I chatted for a few minutes about the armor until even Ryota relaxed and the four of us began to feel like friends.

As Ryota was laughing at something she'd said, I leaned in and touched his elbow. "Excuse me, I just need to visit the washroom."

He patted my hand without sparing me a glance. "Of course, of course."

I backed away silently and slipped out into the hallway. I grinned to myself. Saved by a beauty contestant.

I continued down the empty hall, trying every door and finding most of them locked. The unlocked rooms consisted of a cleaning closet, a powder room, and an empty room with a chalkboard fastened to the wall. There were three rooms stacked with suspicious looking wooden crates, but no more artifacts to be found.

I took the stairs to the next level up but soon realized that the upper floors were not in use. A draft swept across the dusty floors and the walls up here were crumbling, the wood covered in spider webs. Here, the fortress looked as though it had not been touched in a hundred years. I went back down the stairs all the way to the foyer and took the hallway past the great room. I slowed my gait when a few couples came the other direction, keeping my eyes down and acting like I had every right to be wandering the castle alone.

I went through a door into a square courtyard. The moon illuminated an old well in the center. A scraggly garden reached its vines and hedges up the wooden arches to the second level. Circling the courtyard, I poked my head into the next door. Raucous laughter sent me scampering back to the courtyard and on into the next archway. Teetering on my ridiculous platform flipflops, I was sorely tempted to drop them down the well.

Hiding in the shadows, I waited until the laughing voices passed through the courtyard and went toward the great room. Sneaking back through the courtyard, I went through the arch and passed two sets of stairs going in opposite directions.

Just as I was wondering which direction to go in next, a voice startled me.

"Are you lost?"

My heart in my throat, I whirled to see a tall, barrel-chested man approaching. He wore a black suit and held a lit cigar between the first two fingers of his right hand. A quick scan showed no missing fingers. He walked slowly, leisurely, stopping close enough that I could smell his spicy cologne. His hair was clipped very short at the back and his white teeth gleamed. Painfully handsome and confident, he oozed menace like a black scorpion.

If this wasn't Raiden, then I was a real geisha.

I put on a simpering laugh that I hoped didn't sound like I was just a bundle of nerves. "A little," I said. "I was admiring the fortress with Ryota and he had to slip away for a moment."

"Lucky for me," the man said, grinning like he meant it. "I was just going to a meeting and I was wishing for some feminine company. Won't you join me?"

He turned and held out an arm toward the empty hallway.

"Ryota should be—"

"I insist." His voice went dangerously soft.

"Certainly," I said, trying to sound like my voice was dripping honey but suspecting I sounded like a mouse caught in a trap instead.

He held out an elbow, and I took it.

"I'm Yokana," I said, as we walked further into the bowels of the fortress. I steadied myself as I waited for him to confirm that I had just accidentally stumbled upon the owner of the sword I needed to secure my freedom.

He clamped his cigar between his teeth and looked down at me. "Mr. Yukimura. Pleased to meet you."

Chapter Sixteen

"You are lucky, too," Raiden said as we turned down another hallway. The air grew cool and we passed through an arch into another small courtyard.

"Why is that?"

"We will be having a ritual tonight," he said as we took a set of stone stairs up an open tower staircase. "You will be able to experience what only very few guests get to see."

A bad feeling took seed deep in my belly. My mind clambered for a reason to dismiss myself without insulting him.

At the top of the stairs, we walked along a balcony with a wooden railing. Dim lights were visible through the thick paper walls to one side of us. Between every support beam, sturdy paper had been nailed in place to form walls. The pagoda roof's wide overhang protected the paper from the elements. I hadn't seen paper walls since my childhood. A stab of longing for my family pierced my heart. What would they think if they saw me now?

"I love these old Imperial Army fortresses," said Raiden, as we walked. "This one was built after the han system was abolished in 1871. It was an interesting year for Japan. The privilege once given only to the samurai was then open to every male between seventeen and forty in order to bolster the army defenses."

"What privilege was that?" I asked, focusing more on keeping my breathing steady than the conversation with Raiden.

A door slid open as though someone standing at it knew Raiden was coming, and as we stepped into the paper dojo, I couldn't help but gasp.

"The right to bear arms," Raiden said.

Fastened to nearly every beam were racks holding weapons of all kinds. The long katanas the samurai were famous for, wakizashi, and the shaku—daggers and knives. Spiked metal knuckles, throwing stars, long blades with even longer handles called su yari, and iron claws I had heard Toshi refer to as tekko-kagi. These were not unlike weapons that Kito had manufactured with his ovens and molds. If my wakizashi was anywhere in this fortress, it was here.

"I'm bringing an unexpected guest," Raiden said lightheartedly to the more than dozen men who turned to face him. All talk was silenced. "I know you won't mind," he said, addressing an older looking man.

"As you say, Oyabun," answered the man with a drop of his chin.

Raiden strode into the circle of men and they parted as he passed through them. I stood at the door, still in shock, my eyes scanning the vast array of weaponry around me.

"Come," Raiden said.

Only when I became aware that every eye was on me did a realize he'd been speaking to me.

Raiden was already seated in an elaborately carved wooden chair that had been set up on a low platform, on a stage of sorts. There were no other seats in the room.

I crossed the room, sweat dripping down the back of my neck, in spite of the cool evening. *Take small steps. Glide. Do nothing quickly.*

"Sit here, beside me." Raiden gestured to a thin, dirty pillow on the floor.

I lowered myself to my knees as gracefully as I could manage. A difficult task in my layers and layers of kimono. I imagined this was what sausages felt like.

"Don't be anxious," he said quietly. He straightened and flicked his fingers at the older man he'd addressed earlier. "Come, Fujio. Let's hear your proposal and begin."

The crowd of men shifted to allow Fujio to come stand in front of Raiden. They stood off to the side, silently, hands clasped behind backs or arms crossed.

"I have committed offense to my Kumicho," said Fujio, addressing Raiden as 'Grandfather,' his eyes downcast to the floor in front of Raiden, "for which I have come to atone."

The hair on the back of my neck stood up at the name that I had used to address my captor for many decades.

"The offense?" Raiden asked. "So all can hear." His voice was almost jovial.

"I am unable to pay my debt by the agreed upon date, and humbly request an extension."

The room grew quiet. I stole a glance up at Raiden. His eyes narrowed, his fingers stroking his chin. Although he looked thoughtful, I had the impression that he already knew what he wanted—he was being pensive just for show.

"You may have your extension," he said, finally. "But a delay in repaying a debt, especially one as large as yours, will require an answer." He paused, lips apart.

I thought of Inaba and closed my eyes. I knew what was coming and what Raiden had meant by 'ceremony.'

"Yubitsume," said Raiden. As simply as though he'd asked for a coffee, Raiden ordered Fujio to cut off a finger joint.

My eyes flew to Raiden, horrified. Only with great effort did I pull them back down to the floor.

Fujio's face remained impassive, completely void of all expression. He bowed once. There was movement behind me as a man crossed the room and out of my view. He reappeared carrying a small wooden table which he set down in front of Fujio. A small white cloth, no larger than a napkin was produced from his back pocket and laid over the table's surface. He moved off to the side again, where I couldn't see him behind Raiden's chair.

Fujio knelt at the table and sat back on his haunches. He rolled the cuffs of his shirt up his forearms, his movements slow and methodical.

The man who had brought the table reappeared holding a long blade. He held it out with both hands, open flat for Fujio to take. But Fujio put up a palm, declining the blade.

My heart thudded with dread and the cold fingers of disgust wrapped around my spine.

Fujio reached to his belt and pulled out his own knife, one I hadn't noticed as it was hidden in the folds of his clothing. He spread his left hand out flat on the white napkin and the tip of the blade near the end of his pinkie finger. I noticed that he'd already lost the first knuckle of his left pinkie. Fujio had done this before.

I stifled a gasp as he brought the blade down hard. No different than cutting through a sausage. It happened so fast I had no time to look away. The napkin blossomed with red from the wound, but Fujio made no sound of pain. His face remained as it had always been—impassive.

I felt unable to tear my gaze away from the small segment of flesh and bone sitting there on the napkin. The man who'd delivered the table handed Fujio what looked like a bandage. Fujio took it and wrapped up his bleeding stub. Immediately the bandage soaked through with red.

I was certain that every person in the room could hear my heart pounding. A burning sensation hit the back of my throat and I closed my eyes, thinking I might be sick. How did I get here? All of the little muscles around my spine were trembling with anguish for the man who'd been forced to mutilate himself. Sitting there on my knees on the thin mat, I could barely keep my eyes on the floor as

Fujio wrapped up what was left of his pinkie finger in the white cloth and stood. His face had been leeched of color, but still he made no expression of pain.

Fujio approached Raiden solemnly and bowed, holding out the napkin containing his sacrifice. "Thank you, for giving me the opportunity to make amends."

My jaw went slack and I had to snap it closed. *Thank you?*

"Wait," Raiden said, raising his fingertips from the armrest of his chair. "One last thing and you will be absolved of all offense."

Fujio dropped his chin and waited, his eyes on the floor.

Raiden stood up and took off his suit jacket. He stepped down from the platform and strode toward the wall of weaponry, looking it over casually. He unbuttoned the top few buttons of his shirt, undid the cufflinks at his wrists and tossed them to one of the men, who caught them. He turned back to Fujio. "Choose your weapon," he said with a smug smile.

For the first time, Fujio wore an expression other than emptiness and a mirrored vacancy. The shock came and went in a flash, but it was clear as crystal that he had not expected this.

I scanned the other faces in the room and there were a few looks shared among the men, but most kept their faces serene. This was an unusual turn of events. Clearly, Raiden wanted to fight, but what did that mean? To the death? Only until enough blood had been spilled to satisfy him? Fujio had just lost the tip of his finger. Blood dripped onto the floor from the soaked bandage. How was he supposed to wield a sword?

I couldn't watch, and squirmed on my mat, my eyes darting for the door. I struggled to maintain the focus on why I was here as the horrific events unfolded in front of me.

As Fujio walked the wall of weapons, every eye in the room was on his back. Perhaps no one would notice me sneak out. I leaned forward and pushed myself halfway to my feet, moving slowly.

"Stay," Raiden said.

I looked up and caught his eye. His gaze nailed me to the spot like a rail-spike through my spine. His voice was soft, but it was not a request; it was a command.

I knelt again, my mind racing. I used the opportunity to scan the wall of blades, working hard to keep my face neutral and use the time for a focused search instead of watching the grim story unfolding in front of me. Beads of sweat gathered at my temples. My scalp itched and my makeup felt sticky, but I didn't dare scratch or rub my face.

My eyes skimmed each weapon in turn, homing in on short swords. The lighting was dim. A handful of sconces between the beams cast a yellow glow over the scene. Striped and warped shadows fell along the walls and floors.

My eyes fell on a short sword at the top of a rack of weapons. I needed bird vision to be able to tell its color from the distance I was at, but I could tell it was a lighter tone, and I could make out a design of some kind on the sheath. I continued to scan, ignoring the murmurs of conversation going on in the room as the men helped prepare Fujio to fight.

A handful of other wakizashi came to my attention, but I thought that the colors were either too dark, or the designs on them didn't seem to be of trees. I kept going back to the one at the very top of the rack, more and more convinced that it was the sword I was seeking. I stared at it so hard my eyes began to water and I had to blink to clear them.

When I glanced at the men again my heart leapt into my throat.

Raiden had unbuttoned his shirt all the way, exposing the intricate tattoos the yakuza were known for. The front of his chest was tattooed with swimming koi. They spiraled over his shoulders and chest, and swam toward a cluster of chrysanthemum blossoms across his belly. But it wasn't the flowers or the fish that made my blood turn to ice. For in between, evil faces surfacing from the water and droplets falling from their red skin, were three Oni. Raiden dropped his shirt and handed it to one of his men, turning his back toward me.

My skin puckered with goosebumps and I suppressed a shiver of horror. Across his back was a horrifying, three-headed demon. Glaring green eyes, red skin, black talons on its hands and feet, and a spiked club lifted and ready to strike. Cherry blossoms wrapped around its legs and disappeared under the waist of Raiden's belt.

Raiden gestured to Fujio to choose his weapon first. Fujio took a slow turn about the room, scanning. The remainder of his finger had been re-bandaged, though spots of blood had already appeared. His face appeared pale and waxy, even in the yellow light. I thought I saw his hand tremble as he choose a long katana from a bottom row. It was encased in a black lacquer sheath, and gracefully curved. He grasped it by the leather-wrapped handle, unsheathed the silver blade, and held it up for everyone to see. The tip of the blade wavered slightly in Fujio's weakened grip.

Raiden wandered the room more slowly than Fujio had, basking in the eyes taking in the art on his naked torso. He brushed his long fingers against the sheaths of several weapons. The room felt like it was holding its collective breath. I was definitely holding mine and had to consciously remind myself to inhale and exhale.

My eyes darted back to the wakizashi, trying to formulate a plan to take the weapon, but I couldn't focus on the short sword anymore. The tension in the room had risen to an unbearable level. Sweat dampened my lower back and my fingertips were freezing. Was I about to witness a murder? I tucked my hands into the folds of my dress in an effort to warm them.

Raiden reached up high and pulled down a long red sheath encrusted with shiny black stones. Black leather ties dangled from the hilt as he pulled the sword from its sheath. The silver blade reflected a dull gold in the light. It was the size of it that took my breath away. I was certain that stood on its tip next to me, it would tower over me by several inches.

Raiden gripped the hilt in both hands, holding it straight up. His face hardened and focused. His sharp widow's peak hairline cut a jagged frame on his brow and reminded me of portraits of Dracula that I'd seen in art books in the school library. He made sweeping motions with the sword to warm up, rotating his arms and taking light quick steps, like a dancer. His muscles jumped under his skin and the faces of the Oni on his back seemed to come alive. The blade swiped through the air, cutting through the space with sharp whooshes of sound. Had I been Fujio, I would have been filled with terror. As it was, I had tremors of empathetic waves of fright coursing through me on behalf of the older man.

I glanced at Fujio. He was making an effort to appear unintimidated but he swayed slightly on his feet and his eyes were not so impassive as they had been. My heart ached for him. I reminded myself that like Inaba's son, he chose this life. These men gave themselves to the yakuza way. They couldn't be surprised when they found they were in peril because of it.

Chapter Seventeen

Raiden and Fujio moved to the center of the room, standing a few strides apart.

"Ready, ojiisan?" Raiden snarled as he raised the gold-gleaming sword to shoulder height. The blade's cruel light matched the shine of the Oni faces upon the oyabun's trunk.

Fujio took a steadying breath and then, his mouth a grim line, he gave a sharp "Hai!" and it began.

I found myself frozen to the floor, unable to look away as Fujio came on, katana sweeping from low to high with a simple, strong swing. It looked like it was made to cleave from the inner thigh to up under the chin. He never got that far, though.

Raiden stabbed his long-bladed sword downward, arresting the rising blade with a ringing clash. He then stepped into the deflection and snapped an elbow forward to smash across Fujio's brow and send him staggering backwards. The muscles around my spine and in my abdomen quivered with terror as I realized this was no play fight. Raiden didn't follow up with another sword stroke, though. A look of sadistic rapture spread across his face as he watched his prey flounder.

Fujio grunted as he righted himself, blood blackening the gray hair at his temple before tracing a thin crimson bead between the valleys of his weathered face.

"Come on, old tiger," Raiden chuckled, a sound devoid of mirth or sympathy. "Don't you have any teeth left?"

I slumped in relief, thinking that it was over before it had begun, but something flashed through Fujio's pained eyes. Ferocity, or perhaps just the memory of being fierce, rippled over him and he held his katana with new strength, despite the blood that dribbled from his bandaged hand. I wanted to scream at them to stop, but there was too much at stake for me. Instead, I sat frozen in silent horror.

"There they are," Raiden bellowed and the two duelists rushed to meet each other again. Raiden came in with a sweeping swing, a blow easily capable of taking Fujio's head from his shoulders. The older man had come in for a thrust, but seeing the reaper's stroke descending, his stab morphed into a ducking crouch. The long blade whistled by and Raiden gave a surprised *uuumpf* as Fujio surged upward, shoulder first, to deliver a heavy body-check. The oyabun staggered and Fujio, eyes shining with a wild mixture of fear and pride, raised his blade as if for a killing stroke.

A soft gasp escaped from several of the spectators. But the aged yakuza's body betrayed him, his visibly stiff shoulder joints and back slowing him.

Roaring savagely, Raiden drove a fist upward and outward. Fujio's head led the rest of his body in an arched flight backward. It seemed a stunned fraction of eternity before he hit the ground with a heavy thud. Even the timbers seemed to vibrate.

The men around the room visibly winced at the impact.

Raiden was already walking forward, no more playfully stalking by the way he rolled his broad body into the slow gait. Either he did not realize how very close he came to actual defeat or he refused to acknowledge it. He radiated a serpentine arrogance.

Fujio, blood oozing from a mouth twisted out of shape, made to rise, leveraging himself on the katana still gripped in one fist. His eyes were screwed shut and his breath came in wet pants.

Raiden let Fujio stagger to his feet, but only just before his sword licked out in a contemptuous one handed slash. My hands flew to my mouth as a long gash opened the meat of Fujio's forearm. The old man gave a hoarse cry, the sword falling from his mangled limb, and collapsed to one knee. Clutching his savaged arm with his disfigured hand, Fujio choked out a gasp and raised his agonized eyes to meet Raiden's.

Raiden met the stare, unflinching and almost playful, and then laughed again, a cold, hungry sound. The sound seemed like it might have come from the dark water in which the tattooed koi swam; something subterranean, dark and evil.

The oyabun raised his heavy sword to his shoulder, as if preparing for a decapitating stroke, but then delivered a front kick to the old man's chest. Fujio hit the floor hard and slid a foot or so, and then lay still, the puddle of blood around him slowly growing.

Fujio lay upon the floor his hand and arm bleeding freely, but he still clung to life with each hitching breath.

"You are absolved," Raiden said flatly as he turned his back on his broken opponent and moved away. His gaze fell on me as he passed and the grim arrogance in his eyes turned my blood cold. It took everything I had to keep my face impassive and for a second I was thankful for the white paste which hid most of my expression.

As though the words gave permission for the men to move, half a dozen of them went to Fujio's side and helped him up. A towel was bound around his arm and the man half-stumbled and was half-carried from the dojo.

"All of you," Raiden said, and the handful of men standing back made their way toward the door. I moved to get to my feet when he pointed at me and added, "Not you."

I sank back down, swallowing hard, my eyes darting to the wakizashi. Whatever Raiden had in mind for me, it wasn't going to be good. I had to make a move of some kind.

The last of the men left the room, sliding the door shut behind them. Only the sound of Raiden's breathing could be heard. My heart doubled its rhythm and I closed my eyes and steeled myself.

"Stand up," he said, his voice deceptively soft.

I slowly got to my feet, keeping my eyes down. My mind raced and my palms grew clammy.

He spread his long arms wide. The splatters of blood across his face and chest were not his own. The blood on his chest looked like part of his tattoo. The Oni faces rising out from between the koi grinned wickedly at me. A tongue snaked out of one of the Oni's fanged mouths and licked at the splatters of Fujio's blood. *The blood disappeared* into the ugly maw, and the Oni smile grew wider.

I swallowed my own gasp and Inaba's story came rushing back to me in full force. *I began to crave the feeling of blood on my skin.*

"Was I not magnificent?" Raiden asked, taking a step toward me. His tattoos glistened with sweat. "Was I not merciful, in the end?"

Nausea rose in the back of my throat and I swallowed a gag. I kept my eyes down so he couldn't see the disgust, the anger, and the fear simmering there. "Magnificent," I murmured.

He closed the distance between us with a few strides. The smell of sweat and blood and salt swept over me. He put hot, damp palms on either side of my shoulders.

"You are afraid. You do not need to fear me," he said, bringing his lips close to my ear, "as long as you do everything I say, you will be protected. Cherished, even."

The softer sounds in his words hissed out and lingered long under the hard sounds. It was not the voice of a man. He towered over me, his chin easily clearing the top of my geisha wig.

He leaned in close and I was at eye level with an Oni face tattooed just under his collarbone. One piercing Oni eye shut slowly, and reopened.

I cringed and bit my lip so hard I tasted blood. It was my job to remove these evil spirits from this man's body. But I was completely outmatched and incapable. I was small and weak by comparison. Worse, I was full of doubt. I might not make it out of here unscathed.

Raiden's hands slipped around me and went to the ties at my back. Panic exploded in my chest and flapped wildly under my ribs like a caged bird. I took a breath in, my mind racing for what to do. My eyes darted to the wakizashi, visible over Raiden's shoulder. I stood there, rooted to the spot like a petrified tree, as he untied my belt. I felt my dress loosen as the belt fell to the floor. Next he pushed the wig and cap from my head. My own black strands fell loose around my shoulders.

He made a deep humming sound in his throat. "Beautiful," he growled. "You know what I like to do to beautiful things?"

He moved his hands back to my shoulders, his fingertips hooking at the collar of my robe. One tug and the whole thing would fall open and leave me exposed. He bent lower still and I felt the tip of his nose graze my cheekbone. He inhaled deeply.

Then he froze, his face next to mine. His fingers dug into my shoulders hard and he pulled his face back abruptly. His countenance had changed, his eyes were wide with shock and surprise.

"Kin?" He breathed the word out underneath the hum that seemed to have no end as it vibrated from his throat. He took another inhale.

My entire body was trembling now, every nerve and cell screaming to run. I could not leave without that wakizashi, and there was no way this man would let me leave with it, let alone take a step.

"No, not kin. Hanta?" he hissed as he pulled back, amazed. A slow, wicked grin crossed his face. "But you are terrified. I can smell your fear. What kind of Hanta are you that you should fear us?"

As he spoke, his fingers dug into the flesh of my shoulders. Something sharp and pointy emerged from the ends of each finger.

I bit off a cry of pain as the needles poked at me.

"What's wrong with you, Hanta?" His voice descended and became multiple voices in one.

The points at the ends of his fingers punctured my skin and the pain of it jolted me like electricity.

I shimmered and phased into a finch. The desire to chirp and scream was nearly overwhelming, but I stayed silent. As my kimono fell to the floor, the arm hole opened just wide enough for me to dart through it and up toward the ceiling. But there was nowhere to land and I fluttered in panicked circles.

Raiden gasped in surprise and then laughed as he looked up. He abruptly stopped laughing when he saw the small open square between the rafters. I flew toward it but at the last moment turned away. I needed that wakizashi. I wouldn't get another chance.

I fluttered around the room as Raiden craned his head up at me. The room spun and flipped and jumped as I flapped wildly, my brain skittering.

Raiden retrieved his samurai sword, still marked with Fujio's blood. He held it up with both hands. He eyed me and laughed with the voices of many demons.

I had run out of time. One well-placed swing of that sword and he would cleave me in two. Taking on a larger form would put me at greater risk, but I had no choice. I needed to be much stronger than a finch.

Midflight, I phased into an osprey. I screamed down at him and flew straight toward his face. My sudden change caught him by surprise, and the fear in his eyes as he took an abrupt stagger backwards filled me with satisfaction.

He took a panicked swing at me and I barrel-rolled, thankful for my incredibly sharp eyesight and reflexes. I avoided the blade by a hairsbreadth. I shot over his shoulder and went straight for the wakizashi. My talons closed around it and I lifted it from the rack.

Multiple cries of shocked disbelief sounded off behind me. It must have looked to Raiden as though I intended to fight him with a sword, and as a bird. Sounds of confusion from many voices filled the dojo and the voices spoke in some kind of ancient tongue to one another. It was as though the Oni were having a conversation and looking for an explanation for my strange behavior.

My osprey form was too small to carry the sword and the weight of it pulled me down. I twisted awkwardly to the side as the blade swung at me. It bit into the wooden rack just under my right wing. The rack, carrying multiple swords, wobbled and something let go. It tilted onto its side and the swords slid off the rack and clattered to the floor.

I shimmered outward and became an eagle. The sword instantly felt lighter and my powerful wings buoyed me up, but now what? I flapped around the room above Raiden's head, just out of his reach. The dangling rack dislodged from the wall and the whole thing fell down with a crash, Raiden leapt out of its way with a growl of annoyance.

I struggled for space and height. The room wasn't big enough and there were no winds for me to ride, nothing to bear me up. I began to take wide circles, as big as I could make them, but with each rotation I lost height.

Raiden began to laugh again. "What are you going to do now, you stupid creature?" The laughter continued underneath the words. "You want one of our swords? That is what you are going to give your life for? For a moment, we thought a real Hanta had come for us and we were afraid." The backdrop of laughing voices grew louder, even as the speaking voices increased in pitch. "You are no instrument of God. You are no gift from the Æther."

Another circle of the room and I'd be within reach of the razor-sharp blade. The wakizashi was growing heavier, and I felt it slide in my claws. I squeezed the slippery surface tighter, feeling it shift again.

He laughed and lifted his sword. "You are a tragedy."

The words washed over me. I screamed with frustration. I had nothing left to try. Nowhere to go. A roof over my head with a hole too small to escape from, and a host of demons wielding a sword beneath me.

I hefted the sword and closed my talons more firmly around it. With the piercing scream only a raptor is capable of, I used everything in me to shoot towards the wall between two beams. Beak stretched out, wings tucked in, wakizashi dangling from my claws, I hit the wall with all the force and speed I could muster from the small space. The thick paper tore and, nearly dropping the sword, I exploded through to the other side as Raiden's frustrated screams followed me. I hefted the wakizashi to shift my grip and the beautiful sensation of an updraft filled my wings.

Fresh air swept over me. It filled my lungs with oxygen and my whole body with relief. Below me, the courtyard opened up. Riding the wind like a surfer, I climbed high into the sky over the fortress, screaming my relief toward the moon.

I didn't look down. I didn't look back. I shimmered and pushed outward, doubling the reach of my eagle's wings. The burden of the sword lightened again. At this size, I could carry it forever. I climbed higher on powerful wing strokes. The sound of waves crashing on rocks made me want to weep with relief. I was free. I found a warm current. Letting it lift me, I hung in the air with no effort at all. I rode that current all the way to Tottori.

Chapter Eighteen

Grateful for the late hour, as I no longer had my black silk, I transformed on my window sill and nearly fell into my small room. The short sword clattered onto the floor.

Naked and trembling with adrenalin, I lay on the hardwood, listening to my heart slow. The wakizashi lay at my feet. I lay in a crescent moon shape, staring at the blue sheath with its pale pattern. I couldn't allow myself to think too hard about what this meant. The hardest part of the task was done, but it wasn't over yet.

After a few minutes of rest, I got up and closed the window. I turned on the light and wrapped myself in a towel from the shelf in the bathroom. Sitting on the small bed, I considered the item which I had almost died to retrieve. I examined the sheath and the handle. It was a work of stunning craftsmanship. Blue, with a mother of pearl pattern of trees down the length of it. The leather wrapping on the handle had been dyed blue long ago, but it had faded to blue-gray with time and from the oils from the hands of its handlers.

I slid the sword from its sheath. The blade had been oiled and well kept. It was sharp and shiny and had been stamped with a small imprint of chrysanthemum blossoms and curling stems near the hilt. I held it pointed upward and gripped it in both hands. The wakizashi was not nearly as intimidating as the longer samurai swords, and other than its beautiful sheath and imprint of flowers, the sword itself seemed somewhat unremarkable. I wondered why it was so important to Daichi.

Now that I was out of danger, exhaustion settled into my bones and I sheathed the sword, stowed it in the safe, and took a long, hot shower. I washed my face repeatedly. Even though the geisha makeup had gone once I'd phased into a bird, it still felt like it was clinging to my skin. I shampooed my hair three times and soaped and scrubbed my body until it was almost raw.

There were several puncture wounds in both of my shoulders from the pins that Raiden had somehow pushed from his fingertips. I soaped them and gritted my teeth as they stung. I shivered at the memory of the winking Oni face, and the tongue that snaked out to lick up the blood splatters on his skin.

I dried myself off and crawled into bed naked, with my wet hair wrapped up in a towel. The last thought I had before losing consciousness was the hope that no one had seen a large golden eagle carrying a sword land on the windowsill of the hotel, and then disappear inside.

* * *

"What do you mean you want me to stay here?" I said into my mobile, hoping that I'd misunderstood Daichi. "I have the sword. Why can't I leave?"

"Wait for me in Tottori," he said. "I will finish up my business here and come to you as soon as possible."

"I thought you wanted me to bring the wakizashi home to you," I said, raking my hand through my tangled hair. I had fallen asleep with it wet and woken up to a mess of knots in the morning. The puncture wounds on my shoulders felt bruised and tender and I winced as I probed them with the pads of my fingers.

"I never said that." He sounded distant, and there was a bit of static on the line that distorted his voice.

I had no right to ask Daichi to explain himself. I didn't even have the ability to do something against his will. I waited, hoping for more, but the line went quiet. Nothing but the sound of muffled static hummed in my ear as I waited for Daichi to give me more information. He didn't.

"How long will you be?" I asked.

"A few days. I will come as soon as I conclude my business here," he repeated. "I will call you as soon as I arrive in Japan. Don't get into trouble. Make yourself of no notice. Soon, you will have your freedom." The static went silent when he hung up.

I sat on my bed for a long time, bemused. Daichi was old. Far older than any human would ever live without a tamashī. As he liked to remind me, he'd been old when I had run into him in the forest that fateful day. My tamashī was keeping him alive in a state of suspended aging, but it didn't give him superpowers, it just gave him longevity and the indentured servitude of a Hanta. The journey wouldn't be easy on him, so why did he want to come to Japan when I could bring the sword to him?

Shrugging, I got up and put on my last set of clothes—a pair of black pants, a gray cotton button-up with short sleeves, and a simple black jacket with a hood. I had nothing more to do but wait for Daichi's arrival.

I no longer had my black silk, so I looked up the name of a tailor to see if I could commission another wrap. Daichi had been brilliant to think of such a thing, I admitted grudgingly. I took my small purse, dropped in my wallet and cell, pulled on my canvas sneakers, and left the hotel. I left the window open just in case.

The day was humid and still, and I soon doffed my jacket and carried it. I half expected to be recognized by some girl who'd been at the fortress the night before, but my fears were irrational. All of the girls would still be there—playing geisha for their yakuza employers. And even if there had been someone in downtown Tottori who had been there last night, the odds that they would recognize me without the geisha costume and makeup were slim.

I wondered what Raiden and his Oni were thinking about the Hanta who had stolen his wakizashi, or if he'd question the other geisha about the girl in the blue kimono with the crane pattern on it. I shoved thoughts of Raiden out of my mind as I walked to the train station. He didn't deserve to take up any more real estate in my thoughts than he already had. But the niggling idea that I was supposedly powerful enough to rescue Raiden from his possessors never went fully quiet.

I found my way into the shopping district and used my GPS to locate the tailor's shop. I pushed my way into the tiny store and the subtle smell of textiles and dust came to my nose. A small counter was surrounded by bolts and bolts of fabric stacked in deep shelves on every wall.

The voices of two men could be heard talking through a narrow doorway closed only by a curtain. At the sound of the door, the drawn face of a man appeared. He emerged and stood behind the counter, giving me a small bow.

"How can I help you, miss?" he asked, his words thick with the local Tottori accent. He was missing a few teeth from his lower jaw, and he had dark circles around his eyes. Otherwise, he smiled obligingly.

I returned his small head-bow. "I need a simple black robe made. It needs to be one hundred percent silk. Can you do that?"

"Certainly." He nodded. "Do you have a pattern you'd like me to use?"

I shook my head. "Could you work from a drawing? It is not a complicated design."

"If your drawing is good." He turned and pulled down several bolts of black fabric. Laying them across the counter he said, "These are all silk." He produced a box from beneath the countertop and opened it, displaying several spools of thread.

I fingered the fabrics, choosing the thinnest and lightest one.

"That is beautiful silk from China," he said. "It is very delicate, but also strong."

"The lighter the better." I peered into the box of threads. "The thread needs to be one hundred percent silk, too. Which ones of these are silk?"

"Oh." He paused and tapped his chin thoughtfully with a finger. "One minute."

He disappeared behind the curtain and I heard more murmured voices. He reappeared carrying a smaller wooden box. Putting the other one away, he opened the older looking trunk. He took a pair of spectacles from his pocket and searched the jumble of half-empty spools of thread. He retrieved one and perched the glasses on the end of his nose to read the tiny words on the bottom of the spool. "Yes. One hundred percent silk," he said, and handed it to me.

I held it in the light. "Perfect."

He nodded and put the remaining fabrics and spools of thread aside. He rolled open the bolt I had chosen and pulled a notebook out and lay it on top. "For the design," he said, handing me a pencil. He patted his chest pocket. "Where did I put my tape measure—"

I began to draw the simple robe, including the pocket and the little slippers. The man disappeared again and reappeared with a soft, flexible tape. He peered at my drawing and nodded, satisfied. "Very simple. I have made something similar before," he said, "only longer. I've not done these before." He pointed to the slippers. "You need these done in silk as well?"

"Yes, one hundred percent."

He frowned. "They will not last."

"That's okay," I said. "They don't need to—"

I was interrupted when a second man appeared from behind the curtain to watch us talk. My mind skipped a cog when I saw the edges of a tattoo peeking out from under his collar. He was broader and younger than the tailor. He didn't say anything, just watched me through uninterested eyes.

"Um," I scrambled for my train of thought, "the slippers don't need to be sturdy, either. They are mostly for ceremonial purposes." I cleared my throat nervously.

"All right," the tailor said, "if that's what you want." He gestured to a low stool against the wall behind the front entrance. "Step up here, please, and I'll take your measurements. It is for you, I presume?"

I nodded. I stepped up and held my arms out patiently while he measured me, jotting everything down in his notebook. I tried hard not to let the other man's eyes unnerve me, but after the events of the night before, it wasn't easy. Who was this fellow, and why was he just watching the tailor work? Was he yakuza, or was the ink barely visible at the edge of his collar just a regular tattoo?

"How much time do you need?" I asked as the tailor finished my measurements.

"A week should do it," he said.

My heart sank as I stepped down from the stool. "There is no way it could be done faster?" If Daichi happened to arrive tomorrow or the next day, I didn't want to have to be in Tottori any longer than was necessary.

He frowned. "It is an emergency?"

"I would pay a little extra to have it in a few days," I said.

The younger man crossed his arms over his chest, his fingers were adorned with many rings. It wasn't the rings that made my heart stop. He was missing the ends of both of his pinkie fingers. He was yakuza. I comforted myself by thinking that if he knew Raiden, he wouldn't be here, he would be at the fortress with the rest of his brothers. He must be from a different group.

"Very well," the tailor said. "I have access to a few seamstresses. But any sooner than four days is impossible."

I nodded. "Thank you."

He took my cell number and the address of my hotel in case he had questions, and I gave him a down payment of half.

The younger man watched the entire transaction, never taking his eyes off me. I had sweated through my shirt by the time we concluded our business. I left the shop in a hurry.

Chapter Nineteen

I took the train to Furano and stepped off onto the streets of a town I no longer recognized, the town of my youth. Even the shape of the earth under the town had changed. What hadn't changed was the smell of the sea air and the humidity that softened my skin and made my hair feel cool and damp.

I walked the sidewalk of the main street, taking in buildings and homes that had been erected after I'd left. People bustled past me, talking on cell phones, carrying bags and backpacks, all of them walking somewhere with purpose.

My childhood home had been beyond the end of a street that had backed onto a forest, and beyond that, the sea. Multiple trails had led from our yard into the woods. Aimi and I had been able to take our pick. Up to the cliffs, down to the ocean, into the woods, toward the gorge. But now?

I walked slowly, my eyes scanning for some sign of my previous home. There was no indication that my family had ever lived here. Narrow bungalows and apartment buildings, one after the other with a mere few feet between them, spread out before me as far as I could see.

I wandered off the sidewalk and toward a park. It was the first green space I had seen and it bordered a soccer field. Kids kicked a ball around on the field in a chaotic match. More children watched from the stands or played on the swings and playground equipment. I wandered to the stands and took a seat on the warm wooden bench.

I was still watching the kids play when an enormous shadow passed overhead. It was so large I looked up, expecting a low-flying zeppelin. It was too dark and its edges too abrupt to be a cloud. It was also fast-moving. But there was nothing in the sky. My gaze snapped back to the soccer field where the dark shape was still visible. My eyes narrowed and I stood up in the stands. I got up and climbed to the highest seat. None of the kids I passed seemed to have noticed anything strange. I squinted at the shadow as it moved over the field.

My breath caught in my throat. It was the shape of a bird. I looked up again but there was no bird to be seen. All of the hair on my forearms and scalp stood at attention. The shape swept across the green, the span of its wings now visible to me. My jaw went slack. The wingspan covered the entire soccer field, the tips falling across houses and treetops that lined the borders on either side of the park. It glided on until it was out of sight.

I stood on the top step of the stands, my heart rattling and jumping like I'd just run for my life. My eyes strained for another glimpse of the shape, but it was gone. There was only one explanation for a shadow that big, and the fact that no other human around me seemed to notice its presence.

There was another Akuna Hanta here, and they wanted me to know it.

I found their graves by accident.

I made my way back toward the train station in a daze, watching the ground for another enormous shadow that never appeared. When I realized I'd been walking for a long time without paying attention to where I was going, I stopped walking and looked around. I didn't recognize the street anymore. I had not traveled this street on my way from the train station into Furano.

I was about to rifle in my bag for my phone when my eye caught on a narrow walkway between a chain link fence and the back of a row of apartments. A small hand-made sign pointed down the walkway and said Old Furano Cemetery. I crossed the street and took the path. I passed backyards and humming transformers, a few small gardens, and a broken old fountain with cracked paving stones around it.

The cemetery was overgrown with vines and shrubs, the grass hadn't been cut in weeks, and yellow dandelion heads spotted every space between the stones. Square headstones shoved upward from the heaving ground and stood tilted crookedly and covered in moss.

I passed the chain link fence to the entrance. A small sign over the open gate said 1868—1975. This rundown graveyard, barely recognizable and hidden in a back alley, was the burying place of my parents' generation and my own. Surely, I had seen it before when I was a girl, but it was so different looking from the Furano cemetery of my youth. Would my parents be here?

I began a methodical walk to read every headstone and marker I could find, many of them buried in grass. The first name I recognized was Kito's. I stood frozen as my eyes took in the final resting place of Toshi's father. He'd passed in 1947. Vivid memories of the tall imposing man, virile and full of vigor, filled my mind. When I was young, it had seemed impossible that he could ever die.

Dread rolled over me when I passed Toshi's mother's headstone. She had been a quiet, demure woman. Shy, and preferring to stay at home. I never got to know her. She'd passed a year after her husband.

I braced myself as I reached the next stone, but it was not Toshi's. It was a name I didn't recognize. I wandered on, steeling myself against the rush of emotions I would feel if I saw my love's name engraved in a moss-splotched marker. Instead I wandered by several names I didn't recognize, and some I did. I remembered the baker, the man who was always smoking and laughing out in front of his shop. The man who had no teeth whose face had collapsed in on itself, giving the kids of the village reason to laugh and make fun. The old woman who watched the street from her window but never ventured beyond her own yard, always sending her daughter to do her bidding.

It was my mother's headstone that brought me to my knees. I had held it all together until the moment I saw Batya Susumu engraved in the stone. She'd died a mere three years after I had disappeared. Grief washed over me and my head collapsed on my chin. Hot tears welled up in my eyes and spilled down my cheeks. I reached out a hand and put it flat on her name. Why had she died so young? The thick fabric of certainty settled over my shoulders and I knew, as sure as I knew that the sun rises in the East, that my mother had died of a broken heart. Her daughter had vanished without a trace. Had Aimi told her anything? Had she even tried to come after me, to rescue me? Or had she simply let me go and gone on to marry Toshi and be the kind of wife for him that I never could?

"Oh, Mother," I whispered. "I am so sorry. I never wanted to leave you." Tears fell unbidden as birds chirped around me and butterflies and bees darted among the overgrown flowering weeds. A world oblivious to my pain.

I turned my head and my blurry vision made out my father's name on the next marker. He'd passed in 1949, which explained why his stone was a little less rough looking. I wept for him, too, the kind man who had only done his best to give me and Aimi a good life.

I knew I would not find a marker for Aimi. If nothing had happened to kill her, then she'd still be alive. I wondered where she was. I might guess that she was not even in Japan anymore. Modern times made it so easy to travel, and as a Kitsune, she was insatiably curious and opportunistic.

Sobs shook my shoulders as I knelt there at the resting places of my parents. I had never felt so alone in my life.

"It's better to forget those things which are behind," came a deep voice from behind me. "And press on to those things which are ahead."

I gasped and spun around, whipping up to my feet and rubbing the tears from my eyes to clear my vision. The words had been spoken in a dialect not so different from the Japanese I spoke when I was young.

"Don't you think?" The tallest man I had ever seen in my life stood leaning against the metal gatepost. He wore black jeans and a white t-shirt with an unbuttoned, faded black vest. Long, glossy black hair had been pulled half-back from his face and tied up. A high forehead and cheekbones caught the sunlight and threw shadows into the hollows of his cheeks. Tanned skin and a week-old shadow on his jaw suggested a life lived mostly outdoors. The black slashes of his eyebrows gave him a fierce look, but the warm hazel eyes beneath them were soft with compassion. One impossibly long leg was crossed over the other, but it was the pair of white Converse sneakers that made the corner of my mouth lift. I liked him instantly. This man had to be the owner of that enormous shadow that had passed over me at the soccer stadium, and the Hanta who had freed Inaba from his demon. How many Japanese reached this kind of size, or even close to it?

"I thought I was alone," I said, wiping my face and swallowing my tears. A single hiccup escaped.

"Never," he said with a crooked smile. "You're a creature of the Æther. You are never alone." He uncrossed his leg and walked toward me, striding through the long grass. He came to tower over me and gaze at the headstones in front of me. "Who are you crying over, little Hanta?"

"My parents," I said. "I never got to say goodbye to them."

"I'm sorry," he said. "We all have some kind of tragedy in our lives, don't we." He stopped in front of the stones. "Okaasan and Batya Susumu," he read softly.

"How did you find me?" I asked.

His gaze was surprised. "I wasn't looking for you. I happen to be in the area for a target, and I saw you from the sky. I also saw that your tamashī is missing. I have never met a Hanta who lost their tamashī before." He gave a graceful shrug. "I was curious about you."

Curious? I blinked at this. As soon as I had seen him I thought for certain he had come to help me. Now it appeared that this meeting had happened by accident.

"What is your name?" he asked.

"Akiko. And yours?"

"Yuudai. My family name was Yamigu. Not that that matters anymore. Only worldly authorities care about that, and my contact with them is minimal these days." He rolled his eyes. "Thank God for small mercies. What a mess this realm is in."

"You are the Hanta who helped Inaba," I said.

Yuudai's casual behavior was so unexpected that I felt like the world had just tilted off its axis. He was exactly as Inaba had described him physically, but I had expected a much more imposing personality. Instead, he oozed 'boy-next-door.'

"Inaba?" He looked pensive.

"In Kyoto. A yakuza boss with Oni tattoos," I prompted. I was surprised that he couldn't remember the man who had cut all of the ink out of his skin.

Yuudai gave a hearty laugh, showing straight white teeth. "Do you know how many people I have saved that that describes?" He shook his head. "I don't take names. There is no point." He gestured towards the open gate. "If you are finished here, would you like to get some dinner?"

"Um." I blinked at the unexpected invitation. "Yes, I would. But, you said you were here for a target. You have time to go out for a meal?"

"It's not ripe yet," he said, surprising me further.

"Ripe...?" I trailed off, confused.

"And I'm always hungry." He grinned down at me. "Aren't you?"

"I suppose," I murmured, bemused. Truthfully, I was emotionally raw from the discovery of my parents' graves. The last thing on my mind was food but I wasn't going to let the opportunity of spending time with this Hanta slip through my grasp. I followed Yuudai out of the graveyard and down the small alley.

Chapter Twenty

Yuudai ordered enough food to feed six of me. Fried fish and rice dishes, miso soup, rolls of maki, nigiri, and temaki. He also ordered a liter of hot sake and insisted on pouring it for me every time my cup was nearing empty.

"You know I can't pour my own sake, right?" he said around a bite of rice, peering into his empty cup.

"Yes, sorry," I said, picking up the hot bottle by the napkin wrapped around it. "You just drink it faster than anyone else I know."

I filled his cup with the yeasty smelling liquid. I set it down, watched him down it in one gulp, and then take bite after bite of sushi. I wondered if he'd ever get full.

"So, you really didn't find me to help me?" I asked, scooping some rice into my mouth with my chopsticks.

His eyes found mine as he swallowed his mouthful. "I can't help you," he replied matter-of-factly. " I would if I could." He shoved in another mouthful of octopus tentacles and rice.

"Why can't you?" I poured him another cup of sake.

He stopped chewing momentarily. "You really don't know this?"

I shook my head.

He swallowed and shot back the sake. "What happened to you? How did you lose your tamashī?"

I told him about my family, how Aimi and I had been playing in the woods when we'd happened upon Daichi and he'd stolen my tamashī. How I had been his slave ever since. It flowed out easily, with no restriction. Apparently Daichi's command of secrecy didn't hold when it was a Hanta I was addressing. It felt so good to tell my story that I had to fight to keep my emotions from spilling everywhere.

Yuudai didn't take a single bite of food as I described my circumstance. He listened intently and his eyes roamed my face. His brow creased when I told him that Daichi had swallowed my tamashī. "I wonder why he did that?"

Yuudai murmured. "I don't think he needed to swallow it to keep you in his power. Strange choice."

"I guess he was worried about me being able to take it back."

"Yeah, but one command from him and you'd be unable to, anyway. Huh," he scratched his chin. "Go on."

I told him how once I was in Daichi's power, I had been kept in a cage for years on end. It was only in the last decade that he'd allowed me to remain as a human and had me learn English so I could be of use to him.

Yuudai shook his head in horror and wonder. "I wonder why he wanted to stay alive for so long if it was just to rot in some small town in a foreign country," he mused. "And you say now that all you have to do is give Daichi this sword and he will give you your tamashī back?"

I nodded. "He has issued a command that I cannot use any Hanta abilities for anything other than pursuing this one goal."

"And when he gives you a command, you are compelled to follow it."

I nodded again. "It is irresistible. He owns me."

"So you have never actually hunted or unseated a demon before?" Yuudai began to eat again, filling his mouth with rice.

"Never. I have no idea how it's done." I leaned forward. "You can see why I thought you might have come to help me."

Just then our waitress came by to check on us. Most of the food had been consumed by Yuudai, but our rice bowls were still half-full. Yuudai asked for more temaki and another bottle of sake. She bowed and disappeared.

He took a breath. "I would like to help you, and I think, seeing that you know so little of the Hanta life, I can probably tell you some things that you don't yet know. But I can't tell you how to be a Hanta. It would be contradictory to our very nature to explain it to you."

My heart plummeted. "Why is that?"

"Because we operate by faith. Faith is to believe without seeing. If I show you how a Hanta's work is done, then you'll fail at it. You literally won't be able to do it. I will have permanently crippled you. You'll be a faithless Hanta." His brow puckered and his mouth turned down at the corners. It was the most negative expression I had seen him make so far. "And it would be better to be dead than to be faithless."

Frustration bubbled in my blood and the desire to press for details was nearly overwhelming. "Inaba told me that you said you can't kill a demon." I was fishing for information. If he wouldn't tell me how a Hanta did their job, then maybe he'd explain more about our enemies.

He took another bite from his bowl and shook his head. "No, they can't be killed. Not by a Hanta anyway."

"By who?"

He half-shrugged. By now I was getting used to that lift of one shoulder. "That's the business of the Æther, not us. We weren't made to kill them."

"Just to unseat them," I prompted. My rice bowl sat abandoned, getting cold. The sake had warmed my blood.

The waitress returned with a fresh bottle of sake. We thanked her and she took away the empty plates from in front of Yuudai. I noticed her eyes linger on his face and form, on his long limbs. Yuudai didn't notice. He was probably used to the stares. Either that or he was oblivious to them.

I picked up the sake and poured him a fresh cup. "You said that your target wasn't 'ripe,'" I said, setting down the ceramic jug. "What did you mean by that?"

He took a deep breath as though he was starting to get full. His eyes roamed the dishes left in front of us. He snagged the last temaki cone and took a huge bite. I stifled a laugh. The way he ate reminded me of the jocks at the high school, desperate to fill every empty space.

"You're like the world's largest hummingbird. Five minutes from starvation at any given moment," I laughed.

He shot a stuffed-cheeks smile at me and swallowed his temaki. "That's not far from the truth," he said. "You try fueling a body like mine and see how far you get on no food."

"Good point." I had never really noticed that I was any more hungry than my girlfriends. Georjayna ate the most of any of us, but she was nearly six feet tall, so that made sense. Yuudai would tower over Georjie, probably by a good six inches, so it made sense too that he needed thousands of calories to get through a day.

"I'm guessing you've lost your Hanta vision?" Yuudai asked as he lifted a bowl of soup to his lips and took long swallows. He smacked his lips and set it down before eyeing up the waitress as she set down a plate of tuna sashimi laid out in a flower shape.

"I never had it," I said. Aimi had talked about the vision, assuring me that it would come as I matured.

"That sucks," he said. "You were very young when your tamashī was stolen." Five pieces of sashimi disappeared down his throat, he barely chewed. "You can't hunt without it."

"But you didn't answer my question—"

He was already nodding around another mouthful. "Ripe, yes. This is something that you will understand when you get your vision back." He swallowed. His eyes grabbed mine and his face went serious. "What you haven't learned yet, is that demons have a purpose. Yes, they are evil, wicked, horrible creatures that feed on blood and fear and chaos—"

I felt the blood drain from my face at this description.

"But, even wickedness has a reason for being. You can't have light without dark, and the people who get themselves tangled up with demons have become vulnerable to possession by putting themselves in a demon's path. Some deeply deceived people even seek them out because demons can present themselves as a kind of savior."

My head jerked back in surprise. "Why would they do that?"

He cocked a dark eyebrow and raised a finger, "Don't make the mistake of underestimating the power of these entities. They can influence the events that happen in the earthly realm, always through deception. It's all around us. There is a war going on. Humans think the war is with each other, but it's not. Their enemies are not flesh and blood, but demonic entities in high places. The Akuna Hanta were very important at one time, and we are becoming very important yet again. Possessions are increasing, especially with humans who have a lot of political power. Demons have caught on that it's through the elite families of the world that they can have the most influence, and the elite are more than happy to make pacts with them."

"Because the demons make them more powerful?"

"Exactly," he said. "And those humans who have made these pacts are beyond our reach. The Hanta has a responsibility to help humans who have a wish to be freed. But for those who are being used voluntarily in exchange for something like fame or fortune, we can't help them." He shook his head and took another bite.

"So, the ones who are ripe?"

Around a mouthful of rice and vegetables he said, "The host has been through hell with this entity inside them, and only when they are in the worst of it, when they've been brought to their knees, can they be freed." He swallowed, the thick column of his throat moving. "Doing it this way triggers real change in a human heart. It isn't likely that anyone would ever want to make the same mistake again. They were deceived into hosting it, and they have come full circle and now know that demons might lead to a temporary power, but will end only in destruction and death." He raised a finger again. "Until that point, when they are full of regret and desperation to be free," he made two fists and thudded them against his chest. "When their spirit is absolutely wailing, and you can hear it from miles away," his face scrunched up to illustrate the agony the people in this state were experiencing, "spiritually screaming in abject misery." His eyes popped open and he opened both fists at the same time, splaying his fingers outward. His face became a mask of wonder and ecstasy. "Only then can you help them."

I stared at him, mesmerized.

His voice lowered nearly to a whisper. "In that moment, they are ripe. There is nothing that feels better than unseating that evil." His eyes grew wistful, the same way any professional who loves his work might look.

My spine had pushed back against my seat as he had described this. Goosebumps crawled over my flesh. "I'll experience all this when I have my Hanta vision back?"

He nodded and his theatrical face relaxed into its normal chilled-out expression. "More or less." He scooped up a roll of sushi with his chopsticks and into his mouth it went.

"Your wingspan," I said, my mind going back to the enormous shadow that had passed over me.

He swallowed, bumped a fist against his chest and gave a soft burp. "Excuse me." He cringed and looked around, hoping he hadn't offended some innocent passer-by. "That caught your attention, did it?"

"How could it not?" I said, hiding a smile behind my hand. "How can you possibly be that big?"

He chuckled.

"You have some seaweed caught right here," I said, pointing to my teeth to show him where.

"Thanks," he said, and fished it out with his tongue. "Better?" He fake-grinned at me, showing more teeth than there are keys on a piano.

"Beautiful," I said, laughing. The more time I spent with Yuudai, the more I liked him.

"I weigh three hundred pounds," he said. "Birds have hollow bones. Even the largest raptor with a wingspan of ten feet rarely weighs more than two-and-a-half pounds. If I use all my mass..." he shrugged.

I blinked with understanding. "You're as wide as a soccer field?" Why had I never realized this before? I had never tried to be anything larger than a normal-sized bird. I had never had a reason to be bigger, other than big enough to carry the wakizashi. The night before, when I'd increased my size to make the sword easier to carry, I didn't think about pouring all of my fleshly weight into my bird form. How big would the wingspan of a ninety-pound bird be if a bird had hollow bones?

Yuudai gave a cough to dislodge something in his chest. "Bigger." He said it without any pride, just matter-of-factly.

My eyes widened. "Have you ever measured?"

He laughed. "No, why would I do that?"

"But if you had to guess?"

He blew out a breath and closed one eye. "Maybe a thousand meters?"

My jaw dropped. The waitress walked by and I snapped my mouth shut. "Your wings can span a kilometer?" I said in a hushed whisper.

"Yes, or I can be a hummingbird. That's the beauty of being a Hanta." He sat back and surveyed the wreckage of our table. Drippings of sauce dotted the place mats, crumpled napkins sat sucking up leftover broth in empty bowls, stray grains of rice stuck to just about everything. The space in front of me was empty and clean.

"What? You're done?" I said, hardly able to believe it.

After a longing look at the empty dishes, he glanced up and grinned hopefully. "Dessert?"

Chapter Twenty-One

"Where are you staying?" I asked as we stepped out onto the sidewalk. The light was growing dim and the shadows had deepened. I was taken over by a sudden panic that Yuudai was going to leave me alone to wait for Daichi. It knocked the breath from my system just how much I wasn't ready to say goodbye to him. Had I attached to him because he was a Hanta, or because of who he was as a person?

"I rented an apartment in Tottori. You?" We turned and began to walk toward the train station.

"I'm in Tottori, too, at the Gato Hotel," I said.

We walked in silence to the train station, but my mind was anything but quiet. As the trees and mountain-scape slid by through the train windows, I searched for a reason to stay with Yuudai longer. He was the only Hanta I had ever met. He was kind, and fun, and I had nothing to do but wait for Daichi to call and tell me he was here. I dreaded going back to my small hotel room and rotting there while time ticked by.

We stepped off the train together and began to walk toward the center of Tottori.

"I have to go this way," Yuudai said, jerking a thumb in the opposite direction of the Gato Hotel.

I swallowed, brave words dying on my tongue. "Okay," I said.

"Why don't you come with me?" Yuudai said. "We can get an ice cream on the way."

My heart leapt. I'd eat cockroaches if it meant I could stay with Yuudai a little longer. "I'd like that."

"No pressure," Yuudai said, holding up a hand. "Only if you want."

"I want," I said.

Yuudai and I ordered ice cream cups from a small shop in the town center, and I followed him to a tall apartment building with trees and vines and flowers spilling from every balcony. I expected to feel some kind of hesitancy or anxiety at going to the apartment of a man I had just met.

But I trusted Yuudai completely. He was a Hanta. If I couldn't trust another hunter, then who could I trust?

With the spoon in his mouth, Yuudai unlocked his door and opened it for me. The place was breezy and light. The balcony door was open and the white curtains blew into the single room, stirring the leaves of a plant on the table. The largest bed I had ever seen, dressed fully in white sheets, sat in the middle of the wall.

"How did you find a place with a bed that big?" I asked, awed. "All of the beds are always so small."

"It wasn't easy, trust me. I had help." He closed the door and plopped down on the narrow couch at the foot of the bed. "I don't need much, but I hate when my feet dangle off the end of the bed." His face colored. "Spoiled, I know."

I laughed and sat in the chair across from him. "How do you fund your Hanta life, anyway?"

"My wife's business," he said, taking a huge scoop of ice cream.

My smile melted away and there was nothing I could do to stop it. "You're married?" I was shocked on multiple levels. I'd had the impression that he was too busy as a Hanta to be living a human life on the side. And everything about him so far had oozed bachelor. He wore no wedding ring, or any jewelry of any kind as a matter of fact.

"I was," he said. "She left me about six years ago. Can't blame her. Human women need husbands who are present, and I was gone a lot. It was inevitable, really."

"Your ex-wife pays your living expenses?"

"No, but when we split up, we divided everything equally. It was an amiable split, thankfully. She had recently sold a media company that she'd started decades ago. It was worth a fortune. I was a partner in an engineering firm in Tokyo, so I had done well, too." He peered sadly into his empty ice-cream cup and then set it on the small table beside him. "I invested my share of the money in some stocks and it generates more than enough for me. After the split, I quit my job and went Hanta full-time. I only intended to do it full-time for a couple years, but it's been six and—" he leaned back and spread his hands wide as if to say 'here I am'.

"Oh." My ice cream had melted into a puddle and I set it on the coffee table unfinished.

"So, what are you going to do when you get your tamashī back?" Yuudai asked, lacing his fingers together.

The question hit me like a mental wrecking ball. "What?" I sat up straighter.

"When you get your tamashī back, what are you going to do then?" he repeated patiently.

It was like the breath had been knocked from my body. I hadn't thought that far ahead. What *was* I going to do? I had been a slave for so long that I didn't know how to be anything else. "I don't know."

Reality was that Daichi would give it back to me as soon as I gave him the wakizashi, and even that could be a mere handful of days, or even hours away.

Yuudai's brows knitted together with concern. "You don't know?"

I shook my head. Toshi's beautiful face flashed in front of my eyes. "For a long time, it was the desire to get back to my fiancé that kept me waking up every morning. But when so many years passed, and I knew he couldn't possibly be alive anymore..." I trailed off.

Yuudai was watching me intently. "You were engaged?"

I nodded. "Many years ago. So many years." The weight of all the time I had lost pressed down on my shoulders like a jacket with lead in its pockets. Tears threatened for a second time that day. I hadn't wept for my family or for Toshi in such a long time. It seemed that coming home, no matter how much it had changed, was enough to rip open even the oldest scars.

"Don't worry," Yuudai said softly. "When you have your tamashī again, a whole new future full of possibilities will open up to you. Between your human life and your Hanta life, there will be no end of things to do."

I smiled, grateful for his positivity. "What about you? You'll continue hunting?" I said, brushing my eyes to clear them.

"For now," he said. "I'll know if it's ever time to settle in one place again. I always thought it would be nice to have the human experience, kids and everything. I sort of tried that and it didn't work out, but—" He made a face and shrugged. "I think for a Hanta, it is important to know what it's like to live a mundane human life." He leaned back and put his long arms behind his head, stretching. "But for now, I'm never happier than when I'm flying the Æther. Up there, it's so—"

"Pure and perfect," I finished for him. I remembered the feeling of pure love and freedom, of losing the edges of my physical self and feeling like part of the Æther.

Thirty-thousand feet up in the air, nestled somewhere in the earth's thin layer of ozone, was a Hanta's heaven. I was reminded of the cold, empty space I had been so acutely aware of up there and wondered what it would feel like when I had my tamashī back.

"Yeah," he said. "Too bad we can't stay up there forever."

His face split in an enormous yawn, and I yawned sympathetically. Without any presumption in his face or movements, Yuudai got up and took off his vest. He dropped it over the couch back, crawled onto his enormous bed and flopped out straight on his back.

"Sake hitting you?" I got up and stretched my legs. I picked up the ice cream cups and found the garbage under the sink.

Yuudai let out a long sigh with a growl at the end of it. "Just tired. And full."

"I'll let you rest then," I said. It was on the tip of my tongue to ask him for a phone number or an email or something when he cracked an eye open.

"Stay, Akiko," he said. "You know you are safe here." He rolled over to his side and lifted a long arm. "Little Hanta."

Without feeling so much as a twinge of weirdness, I crawled under his arm and lay with my back to his chest. His arm draped over me and out toward the edge of the bed. His body heat melted my bones within minutes and there, under the safety of his wing, I fell asleep.

Chapter Twenty-Two

I knew Yuudai was gone before I opened my eyes. The bed had the empty feeling that I was used to. I rolled over and looked at the dent in his pillow. A folded note lay on the pillowcase.

I sat up and opened the note. His handwriting made me smile. Bold strokes with beautiful curves said: *Stay as long as you want. My home is your home. Gone to check on my target.* He'd scribbled a phone number beneath it and: *In case you're gone when I get back.*

I put the number into my phone and sent him a text so he'd have mine. My head jerked up when something buzzed from a drawer—his phone was here. Of course it was. Yuudai was on wings and had left all of his possessions here. In fact, on closer inspection, his clothing was folded and sitting on a chair and his sneakers tucked underneath. I wondered how he got back into the building. He must hide his key somewhere. A breeze lifted the curtain away from the balcony door. It was unlatched. So maybe he didn't hide a key, just left the apartment open the way I'd left my hotel room open.

Thoughts of doors and windows left open made me think of the wakizashi. I got out of bed and splashed my face with water in the bathroom. I pulled my shoes on and left Yuudai's apartment to go to my own.

On the way, I bought fresh orange juice with pulp and slurped it as I wandered back to my neighborhood. I scanned through texts and photos that my friends had been sending through and saw a photo of Targa and her mother, Mira, dressed to the nines. Targa explained that they were at a party celebrating the conclusion of the salvage dive. I zoomed in on the beautiful mother-daughter pair and squinted at them. It seemed like there was something different about Targa. I focused in on her face. She did look different, paler, but in a smoother and more iridescent way. And her green-blue eyes were brighter, more vibrant. She must have laid a filter over the image.

I smiled to myself as I pounded out a return text to the conversation.

Hi guys. Nice pix, Targa.

Georjie fired back: *SHE LIVES*

Me: *Very funny.*

Targa: *Everything okay? We've been wondering when we'd hear from you.*

I turned the last corner before my hotel, looked up, and almost choked on the juice. I immediately turned around and hid behind the corner. My appetite had gone and my pulse was tripping. The man who had watched me in the tailor's shop was sitting on a bench just a stone's throw from my front door.

I pounded out a last hasty text to the girls: *All okay. Gotta run. Sorry, I only have a few seconds.*

I put my phone away and took another peek around the corner. It couldn't be a coincidence that he was sitting right outside my hotel, three stories below my window. Tottori was way too big for him to just stumble upon this bench and it wasn't a place someone would want to hang out for long, not with all the beautiful parks nearby. He had to be here for me. What other explanation could there be? He had to be connected to Raiden somehow. Paranoia had my mind doing anxiety-ridden gymnastics. Would I even still be alive if I had gone to my hotel last night?

Not only did I have the problem of this stranger sitting outside my door, I had two other problems served on the side. The only way into my room was through the front door as a human, or through the open window as a bird. Raiden knew I was a Hanta. If I became a sparrow I might fly in unnoticed—if I was lucky—but how would I leave carrying my backpack and the wakizashi?

The second problem was that I had to go back to the tailor and pick up my silk robe. If this man wanted to catch me and deliver me back to Raiden, all he had to do was be there when I arrived to pay for it.

I took a walk, pretending to window shop for an hour and hoping the man would be gone by the time I returned. When I got back to the hostel, I peeked around the corner and my stomach dropped. He was still there. Definitely a stake-out.

I made my way back to Yuudai's apartment, formulating a rough plan while I walked. I would need Yuudai's help with it, though, and I wasn't sure how long he'd be gone. I didn't have any choice. I'd have to wait. Not expecting a response, I knocked on his apartment door and was pleasantly surprised when he flung it wide and bathed me with a grin.

"You came back," he said. "I was about to answer your text."

"You're home! How did the job go?"

He waved a hand. "Easy-peasy. When they're ripe, they unseat like popping a cherry off a tree." He stood aside and let me enter the apartment. "What's wrong? You look worried."

I shifted from one foot to the other. "I have a little problem."

He frowned. "What's going on?"

I explained, and I told him my plan.

The shadows had grown longer by the time I made my way back to the hotel. I peeked around the corner and was surprised to see a different man sitting on the bench. My momentary relief dissolved when he raised a cigarette to his lips and a patch of ink on his wrist peeked out from his cuff. They were stalking me in shifts?

I closed my eyes and summoned my courage. In the simple plan that Yuudai and I had worked out, my job was to be the bait. I watched the man smoke until his cigarette was finished. He flicked the butt onto the pavement. He checked his watch, and then pulled out his phone and began scrolling. I waved to the small brown sparrow perched in the treetop beside the bench. It flew across the courtyard and disappeared in through the only open window on the third floor. If the man had noticed, I would have stepped out and distracted him, but he kept his eyes on his phone as Yuudai went through the window. I watched and waited until I saw Yuudai's form behind the glass giving me a thumbs up. He had the sword.

Now for the risky part.

I stepped out into view and walked toward the hotel entrance. Keeping my eyes on my destination and my stride casual, I passed the man sitting on the bench and pretended not to notice him. He froze for just a second with a new unlit cigarette half-way to his lips, then set it between his lips, casually. I felt his eyes track me to the door.

Every hair on my body stood on end as I opened the front door and felt the man behind me get up and follow. I fought down the urge to bolt. There was no one visible behind the front desk, but the office door behind it was open and I heard a shuffling of paper and the sound of a printer.

As the door shut, I strode quickly past the elevator and darted into the stairwell as quietly as I could manage. I heard the front door open behind me. I held the stairwell door so it closed silently. Instead of going up the stairs to my room, I went down the stairs into the basement level. I heard the door above me open, and quick footsteps go up the stairs. I gulped, thinking that if my heart was pounding any louder, my pursuer would be able to hear it.

When the footsteps over my head were three stories up, I sprinted up the stairs on tiptoe and slipped back out through the lobby. I darted out into the small courtyard and down the alley alongside the building.

"Yuudai?" I whispered, feeling moisture gathering in the hollow of my back.

His face appeared from behind a dumpster and he grinned and stood up. He must have just arrived because all he was wearing were pants. The broad expanse of his bare torso made me blink. I made a valiant effort not to stare. He tossed me my backpack and I caught it. The blue sheath of the wakizashi was poking out the top.

I let out all my pent-up breath. "We did it!"

"Easy," he said, yanking his shirt over his head, and slipping his bare feet into his sneakers. "One of the advantages you have from being so petite, and a woman, is that you will constantly be underestimated."

"I couldn't have done it without you, Yuudai. Thank you."

"You're welcome. If they knew what you were capable of, they would have put three or four men on you, and not on rotation but all at once. I doubt Raiden told them what you are. He might risk credibility among his men. Keeping humans thinking the spirit world is just myth is one of their most effective deceptions." He jerked a thumb towards the end of the alley. "Let's jet."

A tall fence blocked off the alley, and we didn't want go through the courtyard and risk being seen. Yuudai took the backpack from me and slung it over his shoulder. He bent down and threaded his fingers together, making a step for me.

Putting my foot into his hands, I was thrown upward. I grabbed the top of the fence and hauled myself over. It was a long drop to the pavement on the other side and I hesitated.

Yuudai pulled himself up easily with his long limbs, threw his legs over the fence and dropped onto the ground. He held his arms up to help me down.

I lowered myself until I felt his hands lock around my shins and then let him take my weight. I dropped into his arms and he set me on my feet. I felt a touch of heat in my cheeks at how natural and pleasant it felt to be against him —like we'd known each other for years. We jogged to the end of the alley and made our way back toward Yuudai's apartment.

I stopped abruptly on the pavement when I realized something. "I haven't paid for the hotel yet," I said.

Yuudai turned to me. "You have a credit card?"

I nodded and we started walking again.

"So, just call them and tell them you had to leave unexpectedly. It'll be fine."

"You don't think those men will grill the staff about me?"

"Akiko," he gave me a look. "Don't put anything past those guys."

I frowned. The hotel staff wouldn't know anything, I just hoped the yakuza men would believe that. But there was another matter pressing on my mind. "I was wondering if I could beg your help with one more thing."

"As long as it's not showing you how to take down a demon, ask away."

"I think that the reason they knew where I was is because I ordered a robe from a tailor in the city center. How the two are connected I don't know, but as the tailor was measuring me one of them came out from the back and watched." I shuddered remembering his cold, calculating look.

"Tattoos?" Yuudai asked.

"I think so. I could only see a little of his wrist. The missing knuckles were what really gave him away."

Yuudai nodded and scuffed his feet as we turned through a park. It was a shortcut to his apartment. "The yakuza are notorious for getting involved in any business they take a fancy to. Maybe the tailor had something going on the side and they're working together, or maybe they're threatening him. Who knows." He looked over at me curiously. "What do you need a robe for?"

"It was Daichi's idea," I said. "It's one hundred percent silk and—"

He stopped walking suddenly, and his eyes widened. "That's absolutely brilliant! How does it work?"

I laughed. "You caught on quick."

He tucked a long lock behind his ear. "I don't know why I have never thought of it."

"So you know that silk is the only substance that doesn't dissolve in the Æther?"

"I don't know if it's the *only* substance, but it's the only one I know of."

"Why doesn't it?"

"Silkworms are creatures of the Æther, too. They're a lot lower in the hierarchy than we are, but still. Daichi didn't explain that to you?"

I shifted my bag from one shoulder to the other. Yuudai took it from me and slung it over his back. It looked like a kid's backpack on him. "Thanks. And no, Daichi never explains things to me."

"So how does it work?"

"I roll it up, tie it around my neck, and wear it like a collar. It gets a little loose at times and if I have to take a really small shape then I would have to stash it somewhere, but it works okay. It's thin and light. It has a pocket I keep slippers in. It probably helps that I'm so tiny. There's not much to it."

"I love it. I'm getting one made. I've flashed my parts at more people than I care to remember. It's amazing I haven't been arrested for indecent exposure yet."

I laughed. Somehow I didn't think most people would mind catching a glimpse of Yuudai in the buff, but still, it was a shock to see a naked person unexpectedly. "Maybe a pair of shorts and a tank top or something?" I suggested. "If you wore a robe like mine I think you might get as much attention as if you were naked. And maybe skip the slippers?" I giggled at the thought of Yuudai scampering down a sidewalk in a thin silk bathrobe and slippers and nothing else. "Nobody warns you about the logistics of being a Hanta." I grinned.

"Tell me about it," he said. "I have stepped and sat in so much stinging nettle over the years, I think my butt will never be the same."

I sputtered a laugh and just then my phone rang. I fished it out of my backpack. "Daichi," I said, putting the phone to my ear. "I'm here."

"I am in Kyoto," Daichi said into my ear. There was a strange hum in the background, a sort of quiet static. Likely because the call was international.

Hearing his voice after so many days of being on my own sent a jolt through my body. Without even thinking about it, my shoulders dropped and my eyes went down. "Yes. I am in Tottori just as you asked. Where should I meet you?"

As he gave me instructions on where to meet him, I came to a halt on the sidewalk. My eyes shuttered closed and the skin across the back of my neck tingled like a ghost from the past had blown on me. "Yes. I know the spot," I said quietly. I wanted to ask 'why there?' but I just said, "I'll be there." And hung up the phone.

Silence hung in the air until Yuudai shifted, his sneakers scraping the pavement. "So?"

"He's in Kyoto," I said, blinking up at him. "I have to meet him at sunrise tomorrow morning." A swell of mixed emotions rushed through me. Terror. Anticipation. Uncertainty. Excitement.

A slow grin spread across Yuudai's face. He flung a long arm across my shoulders as we resumed walking. "You will be a free Hanta by sunrise tomorrow."

"If Daichi keeps his word," I said. Doubt had begun to make all other emotions go rancid. It was too good to be true, too hard to believe, and all things considered, too easy to achieve.

"Where does he want to meet you?" Yuudai asked as we walked up to his apartment building.

"That's the strange thing," I said, chewing my lip and stepping inside as he held the door open. "It's a place that was once very special to me. A clifftop overlooking the ocean."

Chapter Twenty-Three

It was still dark when I stepped off the train in Furano the next morning, but the air was sweet and clean and the birds were announcing the coming of the sun. I had left even earlier than I needed to, just because Furano was so different to me now that it would take some time to orient myself. I didn't even know if the old trails would still be there. My best hope was to head toward the ocean and follow the coast until I figured out which direction the clifftop was in. I'd be in for quite a climb.

All the houses were dark and the streetlights were on, throwing little spotlights on the pavement. I walked through the same suburb as before and headed down an alley between two duplexes. Passing several blocks and drawing closer to the sea, the houses finally thinned and I entered the forest. There were dozens of trails threading through these woods. I stumbled over kid-sized mountain bike jumps and was spooked by more than one tree-fort looming like a black splotch in the treetops. Finally, I pulled out my phone and turned on the flashlight app to help light my way.

Daichi was an old man. Why would he make the exchange in such a remote place, and so hard for him to reach? I half expected to stumble across him somewhere in the bush, lost and tired.

The trail became more rocky and filled with natural steps nearly too big to step up without grunting. By the time the sky turned pink and the woods lightened enough for me to turn off my flashlight, my scalp and clothes were damp with sweat.

A branch snapped behind me and I jumped and turned, scanning the woods. I froze, listening, but the forest had gone silent. These woods had been mine once, but they were so changed that I barely recognized the sounds of my old home. I lifted my backpack to cool my back and kept climbing. A pale light began to penetrate the canopy, dusting everything in a soft glow.

The sound of something heavy off to my right made me freeze, my eyes questing the undergrowth. Some kind of animal, larger than a bird but smaller than a deer, was moving alongside me. I squinted, wishing I could trade my human vision for a raptor's.

Something furry and gray darted from behind a tree and disappeared behind a rock. I let out a breath. It was just a small fox. I kept climbing. A few minutes later I saw the gray fox again, this time his little face appeared from under the leaves of a shrub.

"I knew a fox once," I said to it quietly as I kept walking. "But black and much bigger than you. Crafty, she was." It lowered its face to the ground and I got a glimpse of his body. A solid dove gray, with a patch of mange on its haunches. Even his eyes were the color of gunmetal. It darted away into the underbrush.

I kept hiking and didn't see the fox anymore, but I knew it was around. Every once in a while a twig would break or the leaves would rustle behind me.

I was very close now, and the sound of waves and gulls filled the air. I climbed up over the last of the boulders and stepped out onto the clifftop where I had fallen in love, where I had shared secrets with my sister, where I'd had my first kiss.

I gasped at how much it had changed. The clifftop used to be so wide you could barely throw a rock from one side of it to the other, and so deep that if you stood with your back at the tree line and looked out, you couldn't see any water at all, just clear blue sky.

In the time that I had been gone, half of the cliff had cracked and fallen into the sea. The forest was thicker, bigger, and tangled with vines and undergrowth. The clifftop itself was more worn down and smooth from rain. My eyes fell on an army-green woolen bedroll and a small leather satchel propped against a tree trunk. He'd spent the night here?

Daichi stood at the cliff edge with his back to me, his hands clasped behind him and looking down at the water. But it wasn't how the cliff had changed, or Daichi's presence that filled me with dread. It was the fact that he was dressed in traditional white samurai robes. My hands grew cold and flew to my mouth as a knot of emotion tightened in my chest. I knew what the white robes meant.

He heard my footsteps but didn't turn to face me. I approached the cliff edge and stood there beside him, looking out as the sun cleared the horizon. My eyes were drawn down to the rubble below us. The waves lapped over the rocky beach that looked so different from the one I used to enjoy with Aimi or Toshi. The beach had eroded, and a handful of run-down fishing boats were tied up at posts that never used to be there.

The shock at what Daichi was going to do faded fast. In the time it took to take one full breath, I kicked myself for not realizing sooner that it was what had to be done. It had been on my lips that he didn't need to do this, but of course, I was wrong. If I was going to be free, he had to give me my tamashī back, and my tamashī was inside him. There was no doubt in my mind that Daichi had been a samurai at one time in his life. For him, this would be an honorable death. Samurai of long-ago always carried two swords: the katana for their enemies, and the wakizashi for themselves.

I dropped my backpack from my shoulders and pulled the wakizashi out. He inclined his head slightly in my direction. His expression was peaceful, even pleased. I handed him the short sword.

"You did not fail me." He grasped the sword with both hands and looked down at it. "I have not laid eyes on this sword in a century." He hefted it, and grasped the handle, pulling the blade from its sheath. The metal shone in the sun. He tested the edge with his thumb in a practiced movement, and seemed satisfied with its sharpness.

It was then that I noticed the matching katana threaded through his belt, the same blue sheath inlaid with mother-of-pearl in the shape of trees. Daichi pulled the long sword out and handed it to me.

I blinked at him, confused. Then his request sank in. Samurai who committed seppuku were seconded by a loyal friend. After the warrior cut open his own belly, the friend would decapitate him to end his suffering quickly. I swallowed and stepped back.

"Please don't make me," I whispered. If he commanded me, there would be nothing I could do about it, whether or not I felt capable, I could not deny him an order.

He looked me in the eye. For as long as I had known him he was lined and aged, and his eyes had always had a dead quality to them. No, not dead, grieving. For the first time, they did not appear sad, but relieved.

He simply held the sword out to me and for several breaths, we were statues on a clifftop. He wasn't going to command me, and I realized with a sinking stomach that it was because I had no choice anyway. I wasn't going to let him suffer in agony while he slowly bled to death. Belly-cutting was not a quick way to die.

I grasped the handle of the sword and took it from him. My mouth was void of all moisture and my vision blurred at the edges. Could this be real? Was this really happening? Was I about to decapitate my captor and companion of multiple decades?

Daichi faced me and bowed in thanks, the first time he had ever made the polite gesture toward me. I bowed back.

When he kneeled down at the edge of the cliff, facing out to sea, I backed away to give him privacy. Every muscle in my body was vibrating in fear of what he'd asked of me, what I was about to witness. He pulled an envelope painted with kanji out of his robe and set it on the ground beside him. He picked up a rock and set it on top of the envelope. He untied the belt at his waist and opened his robe down to the belly.

I panicked. I couldn't watch. It was worse than watching Raiden humiliate Fujio, way worse. I turned around and walked back to the forest, stepping far enough inside the woods that Daichi would have the clifftop to himself, and close enough that I could still see his kneeling form at the cliff's edge.

"This can't be real, this can't be real," I whispered, looking down at the weapon in my hand. I pulled the sword from its sheath and held it in both hands, straight up. I took shaky breaths and turned around to face Daichi.

He was still kneeling, his back to me and the wakizashi on the ground at his side. He had his head bowed. I wondered what he was thinking in these last moments. I knew what I was thinking. This was crazy, and not at all where I thought our relationship would end up. When his withered hand reached for the wakizashi, I dropped my eyes. Sweat sprang out all over my body and I slapped a hand over my mouth to choke off a sob.

There was no sound on the breeze. Not a groan of pain or a whimper. When Daichi collapsed to the side it was like watching a silent film.

"Daichi," I meant to scream but it came out as a choked sob. "No." Everything in my body regretted this moment. There must have been another way. Tears blurred my vision and I shook my head and picked up the sword. He was suffering and I had to end it. It would be an act of mercy. Who knew mercy could be so hard, ask so much.

I stepped out from the woods and halted when a bright light flashed at the cliff's edge. A bright white ball of light was hovering over Daichi's frame. My tamashī.

Squinting, I strode forward, raising the katana. But I froze to the spot again when the color of Daichi's neck and ankles went from pink to ashen gray. Then his form crumbled into dust.

The white robe collapsed into a heap and a breeze picked up some of his ashes, swirling them up into the air and out over the water. I lifted my face to the sky, watching what was left of Daichi drift and scatter on the wind.

There was nothing left of him now, nothing but what I held in my memory. Nothing but a white robe, two samurai swords, and some paper. Did that mean he was at peace?

I could have wept with relief. I wouldn't have to raise a sword to him after all. The moment the tamashī left his body, he reverted to the form he should have been in years ago. Ashes to ashes, dust to dust.

I wiped the tears away from my face and crossed the cliff, my hand reaching for the tamashī. A scuffing sound on the rock made me turn as a shadow fell across me.

A violent shove sent me flying sideways. My neck snapped painfully. I screamed with shock and surprise. The katana fell from my grip and clattered on the stones. I skidded across the rock, bruising my shoulder, and stopped dangerously close to the cliff edge.

The light from my tamashī disappeared as a hand closed around it.

I rolled over onto my back, scrambling away from the ledge. Blinking, I looked up at the shape that towered over me and blocked out the sunrise.

The hand holding my tamashī opened and Raiden looked at it. He wore sunglasses, and the light of my tamashī illuminated his face and mirrored in the lenses of his glasses. My throat felt choked with shock. How had he tracked me? My mind flashed back to the hum on the phonecall I'd had with Daichi, and the tailor who had my number. I squeezed my eyes shut and cursed my own sloppiness.

"A Hanta tamashī." He gave an amazed laugh, like he could not believe his good fortune. "I never dreamed it could be as easy as that. Served up on a platter."

"No!" I screamed. My heart had stopped, my brain refused to believe what it was seeing. "Raiden, don't!"

He dropped the tamashī into the pocket of his suit jacket and patted it like it was some rare coin or a banknote.

Fury filled me. Blood rushed to my face and made me feel like my head was going to explode. I scrambled to my feet and went for the katana. A few moments before, I had been having doubts as to whether I could kill, even if it was to ease suffering. Now it was all I could think about. I could not stand to have my freedom snatched away again, this time likely for good. There would be no release from this captivity. The thought of being under the control of a host of Oni, especially after all I had been through, enraged me.

I grabbed the katana and held it up in front of my face, ready for combat. Every nerve was a live-wire. The blade quivered in the air.

"I would rather die than serve you," I seethed. "Give it back to me." My mind raced and I debated turning the blade on myself, since the odds of actually defeating him in combat were zero.

Raiden looked unafraid—bored, even. "Or what?"

I began to turn the blade around, but it was so long and awkward, and handling a sword was so foreign to me that my whole being telegraphed my intention in slow-motion. Raiden spun so fast he was a blur. His foot kicked the sword out of my hand and pain shot through my wrist and up my right arm.

My knees buckled and I landed on my knees. A sob ripped from my throat as the blade clattered and rolled along the clifftop, coming to a stop in the dust and pebbles. A long keening wail came unbidden from my chest and there was nothing I could do to stop it. I was completely alone, helpless, and now the property of my worst enemy. The humiliation and tragedy of it was enough to crush my heart into powder.

"Stop that," Raiden snapped. "Be quiet. And get up."

The sound snapped off in my throat and I was compelled to get to my feet. I couldn't see through the tears in my eyes, nothing but the blue of the sea beyond Raiden and the rising sun in the distance. I stared at the cliff's edge, longing to throw myself over.

"Don't even think about it," Raiden said. He wandered to where Daichi's white robe sat in a heap. He toed the robe open. An ages-old-looking bloodstain had spread over the lap of the fabric, and more dust floated up and swirled into the air. The wakizashi clattered from the folds and onto the rock.

Raiden stooped to pick it up. Examining the blade, it was easy to see that it was shiny and free from blood. Daichi's blood had turned to ash and blown away.

I wanted to scream at him not to touch it, but my throat was a steel trap. The thought of Raiden touching anything of Daichi's was abhorrent. Strange, since Daichi had been my captor for so long. In that moment I admitted to myself that I had come to care for him in spite of our situation.

"Was it worth it, little Hanta?" he asked, sheathing the wakizashi. He laughed. "You belong to me now."

But just as suddenly, Raiden stopped laughing, and his gaze locked on the woods behind me. I turned.

A man stood just outside the forest. His black hair was tied half-back, and he wore a simple, button-up shirt, with a thick fabric belt wrapped around his waist. A katana with a red leather-wrapped handle was tucked into his belt. He looked exactly as he had the last time I saw him, just as beautiful, just as strong, and I knew I was having visions. I had finally become unhinged and couldn't handle what had just happened.

I had to be hallucinating. Because Toshi was dead.

Chapter Twenty-Four

My heart stopped and then tripled its speed. I felt like I couldn't open my eyes wide enough—I only wanted to stare at my beloved from decades past. I shook my head and squeezed my eyes shut, trying to clear the hallucination. But when I opened my eyes, he was still there.

"She is not yours," Toshi said quietly, his eyes never leaving Raiden's. "She will never be yours."

Raiden bared his teeth in what might have passed for a smile on any other face. "Who are you?" he barked. "An idiot from the village?"

"Return her tamashī," Toshi commanded. "And do it quickly."

Toshi's hand rested on the katana tucked into the broad sash around his waist. Except for the weapon and embroidered band, the man, so slight and youthful, would have been commonplace in a dozen Kyoto campuses or bars. It was his stillness—his lethal, earnest placidity—which made Raiden pause.

Toshi was no hallucination. However impossible, he was here.

My eyes flashed back to Raiden. Taller, wider, stronger. I had seen the brutality of Raiden's heart. He would kill Toshi as soon as look at him.

Raiden's smile widened, catapulting his face to those same demonic proportions I remembered from the night at the fortress. With a speed telling of years of practice, the towering oyabun drew a handgun from the shoulder rig beneath his suit coat. The gun, a metal projection of its owner in steel and polymer, eyed Toshi from beneath its master's grin.

"Or what," Raiden drawled, his free hand removing and then tucking the sunglasses inside his coat. He was only slightly less monstrous without the insectile lenses.

I wanted to scream at Toshi to run. Every muscle in my body tightened in terrible anticipation of the sound of a gunshot and Toshi's body slumping to the rock.

With deliberate slowness, Toshi adjusted his stance, feet spreading and weight shifting forward onto his toes. He adjusted the angle of the sheathed katana like a master steersman handling the tiller. He cocked his head ever so slightly, the movement a clear challenge.

My eyes darted back and forth between the two men and I could almost see the communication that passed between them. Toshi had thrown down a gauntlet, something that Raiden's ego could not deny, even if he could simply pull the trigger and be done with his challenger for good.

The oyabun growled deep in his throat. He rotated the pistol in his fist, a pendulum swaying with fatal whimsy.

Toshi did not move, not even seeming to notice that death was ready to fly from the pistol's blue steel hive.

Raiden laughed, and then with a *sh-h-hrik, k-klick*, the gun's magazine and a formerly chambered round fell to the pebbled clifftop, followed by the louder clatter of the gun itself.

"This should be fun," Raiden said, and I could once again hear the voice of the Oni surfacing. The softer sounds hissed out underneath the words and lingered long in the air like a growl. He shucked out of his suit coat and shoulder holster. Taking his time, he unbuttoned his white shirt. The Oni tattoos shone bright and fearsome in the sunlight.

I watched his jacket fall to the earth. Everything in me strained toward the tamashī in the pocket, but my feet were rooted to the ground just as solidly as my voice was locked down. I looked toward Toshi, trying to tell him that I could help, if only I could get to what was in that coat pocket.

Toshi remained defiant, staring at Raiden in immobile tranquility. My heart burst with love for him and the courage he displayed in the face of such a deadly opponent.

Raiden bent and scooped up the katana Daichi had left behind, weighing it in his hands as if taking its measure. He lifted the sword in both hands. The long blade extended from just above his widow's peak like a gleaming horn of steel. Arms upraised in an aggressive stance, his tattoos were on full display. The koi bodies undulated sleekly across his broad chest. The muscles moving beneath his skin set the Oni faces to laughing. On any normal man, the movement would be just an illusion, but on Raiden, the demons' visages moved just enough to make an opponent do a double-take.

Toshi continued to stare, not reacting to the hideous display before him.

Raiden's laugh became a snarling roar as he launched himself across the distance. Toshi did not advance and did not retreat; in fact, he did not move at all.

My throat swelled with the words clawing to get out, pressure building in my neck and face. I couldn't watch, but I couldn't look away.

Raiden's feet hammered the hard ground, leather dress shoes scattering dust and pebbles in his wake. The space between them had seemed so great, but in a breathless heartbeat Raiden descended on Toshi with a stroke that would have cleaved him from shoulder to groin. In one blink it would all be over.

But Toshi was not there—at least not where the blade descended. He curled back on his haunches, just enough to let the scything blade pass within inches of his face.

Raiden's eyes flickered with surprise, but his fearsome reputation was not built just on looking impressive, and with a rising *kiai* he reversed his strike in an impressive swallow-tail cut. The blow was wasted when Toshi pivoted on his forward foot and the blade hissed upward in a harmless, frustrated *whoosh.*

The oyabun had no time to wallow in his irritation as Toshi's blade licked out. Raiden just managed to swing his blade around to guide the stroke away from his throat.

For the briefest moment, Toshi and Raiden froze with their faces close together and I could see the understanding pass between them. Toshi's fierce glare and tiny smile was full of meaning.

My turn, he seemed to be saying.

Raiden shoved against the blade near his throat with a snarl and Toshi let him. Toshi's katana, lighter and quicker, spun wide and then darted for a low slash across the Raiden's shins. Raiden's height worked against him, and all he could do was dance backward from the serpent tongue of bright steel. Toshi did not advance so much as a single step, and his quiet poise must have stung Raiden more than a thousand insults.

Raiden's dark eyes smoldered. He prowled back and forth a few paces away, blade held level. Suddenly, he kicked off his dress shoes and bent and ripped off his socks. His bare feet settled into the dirt. He straightened and dropped his chin, ready for more. Finally he was taking Toshi seriously. With an eye-stinging flash of sunlight from his katana, Raiden renewed his assault.

With his longer, heavier sword, Raiden began a series of probing jabs and swipes. With the advantage of his greater reach, Raiden had a better shot at the more vulnerable targets—throat, armpit, groin—but each time Toshi's blade set the thrust aside. The men shifted and moved across the clifftop together like dancers. Raiden put more of his weight behind the stabs, drawing on the strength of his shoulders and back. The red-skinned demon tattoo across his spine flexed and bulged grotesquely with each thrust, green eyes winking and flashing, thirsty for Toshi's blood.

Under such a punishing onslaught, Toshi danced and glided, each step taken just in time to avoid Raiden's katana. Feet snapping and sliding across the loose ground, casting the rest of his poised body this way and that, away from the hungry tongue of metal, now desperate to have a taste of him.

Toshi had nearly worked himself to a place with his back to the cliff when Raiden over-extended a lunging stab. Raiden's bare feet skittered across the chipped stones. With a swift precision which made it seem like Toshi had expected the stumble all along, his katana hissed through the air, trailing blood. It had happened so quickly that I didn't even see it; I only knew Toshi's blade had struck when Raiden cried out and recoiled, cradling his wounded arm to his chest. Raiden swung his katana one-handed to fend off Toshi, but the strokes were slow and ill-aimed. Toshi, seeing his chance, uncoiled like a striking cobra.

Katana singing through the air, he drove Raiden back toward the forest. Raiden parried, but the strikes came so fast and smooth that for most of them it was all that he could do just to keep himself lunging and lurching away. When he was too slow, Toshi's razored edge took another little sip of his life, hot and red. An Oni face upon his belly lost an eye to the pass of Toshi's blade.

Raiden's teeth flashed as he bit back a scream.

Rage and fear gave Raiden a burst of hateful quickness, and he threw his bulk inside the guard of Toshi's katana. A rip appeared in Toshi's shirt and blood stained the shredded fabric. Raiden spun on his heel and delivered a crushing back kick to the side of Toshi's belly.

My neck felt as though it was going to burst with the words and screams bottled up inside me. Toshi flew to the side, gasping for air as he folded around his stomach. Still he kept his feet, and his katana, though wavering, held its pointed vigil for its master.

Raiden scrambled across his newly opened avenue to the cliffside. Dirty feet carried him out of reach. Toshi, his face flushing at his enemy's cowardice, moved to follow, albeit more gingerly than before. When he realized that Raiden was arrowing toward the discarded pistol, Toshi leapt after Raiden like a big cat closing in for the kill.

Raiden scooped up the handgun, but he fumbled as he tried to ram the clip home with his injured arm. Toshi came hot on his heels, blade raised before him for a final, head-severing slash. Only instinct saved Raiden as he threw himself to the ground and Toshi's katana whistled overhead.

Raiden snatched Daichi's fallen kimono and threw it violently into Toshi's face. The fabric wrapped around Toshi's head and Toshi danced backward, clawing to remove it. Dust and ash fluffed up into the sky. Toshi threw the fabric free with a flustered grunt, but he had to pause to blink ash from his eyes.

"Koshinuke!" Toshi spat at Raiden's cowardice.

The clip slid home and, growling curses, Raiden worked the slide to chamber a round. Toshi's vision cleared and his whole body snapped to face the earth-bound foe, who swept the pistol upward.

The pistol barked and the katana sang out. The explosion from the gun made my whole body jolt like I'd been struck with lightning.

Raiden screamed as his horrified eyes beheld the bleeding stump just below his wrist. He drew in a shuddering breath to shriek again, but Toshi's blade flashed out again and the cry transformed into a wet gurgle.

Raiden groped weakly at his throat with his remaining hand. Sounds burbled and popped from between his fingers for a few pained heartbeats, and then his body slumped back. His open eyes looked dully to the sky.

Toshi drew a shaky breath, and his eyes swept downward to the red line across his chest. Bright blood poured from the wound and a shiver of pain shook his torso. His knees seemed to buckle, but with a gasp, he leaned on his katana and stayed on his feet.

With my captor's passing, my locked jaw opened and every frozen muscle flooded with energy. A cry ripped from my throat, layered and bursting with every sound I had tried to make since Toshi had appeared from the trees. I leapt forward as Toshi turned to me and opened his arms.

He grunted as we collided and his arms closed tight around me. He was real. He was alive. He was here. My mind skittered for purchase on this new reality.

"Akiko," he sighed, riding through another agonized breath.

I pulled back and looked down between us at the blood spreading on his tunic and darkening my black sweater. I looked back up at his face, my lips trembling and sucking in air. My hands shook so violently I could hardly control them. "You're hurt," I gasped.

"It's all right." He let go of me to approach Raiden's jacket. He reached into the suitcoat pocket and retrieved my tamashī. His face lit up and he squinted until he closed the light wholly in his hand. He returned to me and held his closed hand out, palm down. "I believe this is yours."

Chapter Twenty-Five

I lifted a trembling hand and Toshi passed my tamashī to me. I opened my palm and the bright white-blue light glittered like a star in my left hand. With a shuddering breath, I put my right palm over the tamashī. It melted into my skin and we watched as it trailed up my right arm and into my chest. My heart glowed brightly one last time as my tamashī settled back into its rightful home for the first time in decades.

Tears flowed freely down my face. The years of servitude dropped away from me like heavy ropes falling off my shoulders and the warm, bracing feeling of freedom filled my whole being. For the first time since I was a teenager, I was not under the control of someone else.

My eyes misted as I looked up at Toshi. Even through his pain, love filled his eyes and I could see the relief settle over him.

"How?" I breathed.

His gaze settled on something behind me and I turned to see the mangy gray fox creep from the woods. Its head was low, its gunmetal eyes on us. It sat on its haunches and its tail curled around its paws.

I looked back at Toshi, my eyes widening with surprise and confusion.

"You don't recognize her?" he said, the corners of his mouth lifting slightly.

"Her?" My gaze snapped back to the fox. I gasped as his meaning sank in. "Aimi? It can't be!"

The fox dipped her head, her eyes on mine. She dropped down to her belly and rested her jaw against the stone. She whuffed a sigh out into the dust and a cloud blew up in front of her.

"But, Aimi is black, and she has green eyes. This can't be her." My mind felt shattered in pieces like a jigsaw puzzle.

"A Kitsune without a tamashī turns gray," Toshi said. "With all of the winged shapes you must have taken for your captor over the years, did you not notice that all of your forms were gray?"

I shook my head and my mouth dropped open in protest. But...he was right. A flashwork of memories played vividly through my brain. The reflection of my falcon self over a smooth lake, a flash of my pigeon self in a window over a mall in Kyoto, and my small hopping sparrow against the glass of an open window. All of them—gray.

I turned to the fox, flooded with so many emotions I thought I would burst. Elation, shame, relief. "Aimi," I said, stooping to the earth.

The gray fox bolted toward my outstretched arms and barreled into my chest. My arms closed around her warm body as tears coursed down my face. An overjoyed groan became a whine of barely contained emotion as Aimi rubbed her face against mine and licked my jaw and ear. I covered her little face with kisses and stroked her soft ears back against her head. She licked the tears from my cheeks, her whines peaking with whistles. Her whole body shook and trembled, just like mine did.

"Become a woman so I can see you," I said. "So I can hug you, and we can talk."

She only whined again, deep in her throat. Her gray eyes looked into mine and they seemed filled with sadness.

"She can't," Toshi said from behind us. "Not until I give her this back. Giving away a tamashī seems to mean something different for a Kitsune. She has been in her fox form since 1923."

I turned to see him holding out a glowing yellow ball nestled in the mouth of a small red silk bag. At once the meaning hit me and my limbs froze with shock. Of course. I shouldn't be shocked. How else could Toshi be alive? Aimi had given him her tamashī.

"Why did you do this?" I asked both of them, looking from one face I loved to another. My heart backed up against my spine as though it was afraid to hear the answer.

Toshi smiled. "Why do you think, Akiko? We did it for you. We've been looking for you, waiting for you. We knew of no other way to help you."

I looked back at Aimi's little fox face and the realization of what she had sacrificed for me, what they had both sacrificed for me, hit me like a locomotive. I put my forehead against hers and tears flowed down my face. Shame burned deep in my belly. I had imagined Aimi might even be happy that I was out of the way, that she could have Toshi for herself. How could I have imagined such a thing? Aimi had kept Toshi alive all these years, and had sacrificed her ability to take her human form, not to mention her free will.

I lifted my face to see Toshi kneel beside me. He held his tunic against his cut.

"All these years? All this time? You've been alive," I whispered.

Toshi exhaled. "I have so many questions. Like where did you disappear to, and who it was that took you. We tracked him to the port of Kitakyushu, and there we lost you and have been looking for you ever since." He laced his fingers through mine. He must have seen the agony in my face for he brushed my hair behind my ear and said, "Don't let it upset you. Time can pass differently for a human with a tamashī in his possession."

The sun traveled high into the sky and the heat of the day warmed us as Toshi and I talked, there on the cliff that we had fallen in love on so long ago. Aimi curled up at my side and I stroked her fur and her ears. She listened as Toshi and I talked, Toshi holding a hand to his wound. I made to bind him, but he stopped me, urging me to tell my story.

I told them of Daichi, of how he had taken me on a ship and we had sailed for what seemed like forever, only stopping for a short time before moving on. How he kept me in bird form for so long that I hadn't even known what year it was when he finally let me become human again, and how stunned I had been to learn that we were in Canada. How we'd ended up in a massive country with seemingly endless wilderness, and brutally cold winters. I told them of how I learned the way of life, and eventually made friends who had come to mean the world to me.

I told them how Daichi slowly allowed me to be human for longer periods of time, likely realizing that I was of much more use to him that way. He hired me a tutor to learn English, though he'd never deigned to learn it himself. How he adapted to technology over the years and spent more and more time on his laptop, never allowing me in on his desires until the time came that suited him. I became his go-between for our North American life. I was not permitted to ask him questions, nor did he ever ask for my opinion. Eventually, likely because I'd grown bored running errands for him, he'd allowed me to register in high school, and there I had made my first friends. I'd been commanded to lie to them, to tell them some fictitious story about how my parents had died from a contagious disease that had swept through our village, and that we'd come to Canada because I was half-Canadian already. The lies Daichi wove around us trapped us both into a life of solitude. Targa, Georjayna, and Saxony had become the only spots of happiness in my life, and I was only allowed to see them when it suited Daichi.

The sun arched over us as my story spilled out, pouring from me in waves of emotion until I was all used up and out of words. The three of us sat huddled close together, Toshi's arm wrapped around my shoulder and Aimi leaning into my side, until Toshi took a breath. Dread for what I knew he was going to say filled my gut like lead.

"It's time I returned this to her, don't you think?" Toshi said, holding out the red silk bag containing Aimi's tamashī. I looked at it, and fresh tears rolled down my cheeks, soaking my lap and Aimi's fur. She craned her neck to look up at us, her ears perked.

I pushed my tamashī down my arm and brought the star to my right palm. I held it out to Toshi and looked at him. "Please," I said, my voice breaking. "I only just got you back. Stay with me."

Toshi's face melted with love but he shook his head. "You know that I would never take your freedom from you, Akiko." He curled my fingers tightly around my tamashī and it melted back into my skin.

We hugged one another fiercely and he kissed me. He brushed my tears away and held my face in his palms. "Sometimes we know from very young what we were born for. Even when I was throwing bugs in your hair when we were children, I knew that I was put here for you."

I choked back a sob as he held the red silk bag in front of us and opened it. The yellow glow sat in the puddled fabric, edgeless and bright. Aimi stepped over me and into

Toshi's lap, licking his face. He laughed and said, "Good-bye, my companion. I wish you an eternity of happiness now that our task is completed." He closed his eyes and pressed the yellow star to the fox's fuzzy forehead. It melted into her, glowing from deep inside before fading away and disappearing. She backed up with a whine in her throat.

Toshi's form froze and lost all color. I could still see the smile playing at his lips as a breeze kicked up and then he dissolved into dust. He swirled around us in a spiral and was swept into the sky and out over the ocean, his clothing collapsing into a pile next to me. I put a hand on the soft fabric, the shell that had held him only a moment before. The blood that had stained the front of his shirt turned dark and looked decades old. Ash and dust puddled in the clothing and I picked them up and freed Toshi's remains.

"Good-bye, my love," I whispered, watching the last of him disappear.

The sound of a footstep made me turn. Aimi stood there with only Raiden's suit jacket draped around her. Her long, slender legs poked out from the black coat and her hair, black once again and hanging long to her waist, blew around her in the wind.

"Hello, sister," she said.

Chapter Twenty-Six

As I got to my feet, the skin all down my left side began to prickle. I frowned and rubbed up and down my arm to try and get rid of the feeling. The prickling intensified and swept to the other side of my body. A humming like a swarm of bees only much deeper and darker sounding filled my mind. I grimaced and put my hands to my head.

"What is it?" Aimi's voice sounded far away and slow, like an old recording.

"Wait," I said, shaking my head.

My gaze darted to Raiden's still form. I had forgotten his body was even there. I clenched my teeth as the humming in my head increased. Like a shark could smell blood in the water, I could sense the rotting sulfurous presence of evil. I clenched my teeth against the roiling in my belly. The Oni.

"Come on." I seethed with anticipation. I barely recognized the sound of my own voice. Instinctively, I phased into a falcon and climbed free of my clothing. The moment I had my Hanta vision, a second dimension opened up before me, peeling back like a thin layer of onion skin. The membrane between the material dimension and the one I could now see was as fragile and yet as strong as a spider's web.

The buzzing increased and became a long, low never-ending hum. The Oni faces tattooed on Raiden's skin began to stretch and distort, like they were painted on plastic wrap and concealing a nest of snakes. Roiling under the surface, the Oni pushed, and holes burst through the warped tattoo images. Through the holes, dark amorphous blobs of spirit strained to exit. Six Oni leeched from Raiden's form, stretching and pulling to extract themselves from their fleshy tomb. Shifting shapes of demonic intent, the Oni writhed and stretched, seeking to escape and find a new host.

In the distance, in every direction of land, I could see thin columns of spinning light reaching up from the earth to the sky, so far up that they disappeared from view. It wasn't the time to figure out what I was seeing in the distance, though. I had Oni to unseat. I spread my wings and took off, climbing straight up into the sky. From high above, I could see shape of the demon spirits growing and increasing in size. I screamed a shrill cry and pushed all of my bulk outward. My wingspan expanded in both directions and I circled the cliff looking down at my own massive shadow.

My eyes caught Aimi's form, staring up at me and shielding her eyes from the sun. I was a flesh and blood bird, huge and impossibly loud as another piercing cry tore across the sky. But my prey was not flesh and blood.

The first spirit broke free of Raiden's body. Morphing as it spiraled, its shape shifted from an evil yawning face to two sharp curved claws, and then melted back into a formless shadow.

With a scream I dove toward it, my massive talons outstretched. The moment before I clutched the Oni, my body shimmered and warmth swept over me. My flesh and bone transformed as it passed from the earthly dimension into a spiritual one. I understood in that moment what Yuudai had been talking about when he said Hantas hunted by faith. The spirit form was given to me, just when I needed it. My talons closed around the demon in a death grip, puncturing and holding fast as it writhed and fought. An otherworldly scream of anger sounded off in my mind.

Aimi's eyes widened and she began to call my name, frantically searching the skies for the colossal bird who had been there a moment before. I was there all the same, the Oni yanking and jerking in an effort to free itself from my Hanta talons. Wraithlike screeches filled my mind and made my head throb.

Another Oni demon pulled free of its tomb and became a long, thin worm, making its way down the cliff toward the beach where fishermen were pulling up to the dock with their catch. I dove again, reaching my other claw out and snapping it closed around the Oni. It thrashed like the other, whipping and screaming and wrapping its long body around my leg. Both Oni were twisting and straining to free themselves. I swooped upward, realizing my disadvantage as the four remaining Oni struggled, nearly free from Raiden's corpse.

I dove again. Pinning my wings back against my body, I shot straight down at the demons. I impaled the two Oni in my claws deeply with a single talon, jamming them on firmly as the ground swelled up to meet me. My talons opened wide for the others. I sank my nails into the remaining spirits.

Everything went dark as I flew down into the earth. I felt my claws puncture the demons in multiple places and drag them from Raiden's body. They stretched and screamed until they snapped free, and the impetus from their release flung me even deeper into the earth like a slingshot.

Down, down, down I flew, my spirit wings flapping and my talons holding the Oni fast. My Hanta body jerked as the Oni struggled against me. I doubled my efforts. All down through the rock and minerals and layers of sediment, I felt no material barrier. I could smell the oxygen even in the earth, and I noticed when the oxygen began to thin and when the heat began to increase.

Through groundwater and layers of compressed earth and oil my spirit wings took us, my talons locked shut with my prey. The demons cried a sound I had never heard before, like a rusty scream with a thousand whispers inside it. As the oxygen here thinned, my wings began to tire. We passed into deep subterranean earth where the heat would be unbearable and there was no life. Not even bacteria lived here. Still I continued to fly straight down with everything that I had in me, my massive spirit wings pounding a smooth rhythm.

When my body was crying out for oxygen and I felt I could go no further, I banked upward and opened my talons, throwing the Oni deeper into this Æther-deprived wasteland. Violent screams of frustration echoed around me and grew faint.

I turned upward and began to climb. As I went through the layers of soil and could sense oxygen returning, my strength grew. My wings pounded, gaining energy and increasing my speed. The moment I exploded up from the ground, my flesh and bone form returned to me, a shift that was not in my control but was given by the Æther.

I gave a piercing cry and shrank down to normal size, spiraling over the cliffside.

Aimi spotted me and the worry in her face disappeared. She closed her eyes for a moment in relief. I descended to the clifftop and landed, ruffling my feathers.

I phased back to human, my chest heaving. I fell to my knees and then to my side and rolled over onto my back, naked in the dust and pebbles. I squinted up at the blue sky and sucked in deep breaths. Slowly, my heartbeat went back to normal. I turned my head and saw Raiden's body. I sensed nothing, just a quiet corpse encrusted with dried blood. The Oni tattoos on his chest were dull and unremarkable.

Aimi's shadow fell over me. Silhouetted against the sun, she dropped my clothing on my stomach and stood back. Her hands went to her hips. "Are you okay?"

"Yes," I said. "I'm more than okay." I got up, dusted myself off, and began to dress.

"That was terrifying," Aimi said, matter-of-factly. "When you disappeared, I didn't know what to think. I can't disappear like that. At least, as far as I know."

"I didn't know that I could, either."

"How did you do it?"

"I didn't. The Æther did it." I pulled my shirt down and looked at Aimi. "What you always said about us being creatures of faith, that the Æther would give us what we needed in the moment that we needed it, you were right. As a flesh and blood bird, there would be nothing I could have done about those Oni, but in spirit form," I smiled, "they aren't so terrifying."

She smiled back. "Not to you. You're a Hanta. But for a human—"

We both looked down at Raiden's corpse. I frowned. "If they open the doors, even unknowingly—"

"They are defenseless," Aimi finished my thought. She looked up at me. "What did you do with them?"

"I trapped them deep underground."

Her face brightened. "Of course! No oxygen, no Æther! They'll be impotent down there." She paused. "Forever?"

I frowned. "I guess as long as they have no oxygen, they have no strength."

"Let's hope no one decides to dig for oil here, then."

"Somehow, I don't think there's any danger of that," I smiled. I didn't know how many miles down I took them, but I knew without a doubt it was farther than any human would ever have cause to dig.

"Yeah. Oh, by the way..." She walked over to a stone sitting at the edge of the cliff and bent down to move it. She retrieved an envelope and handed it to me. "This is addressed to you."

Chapter Twenty-Seven

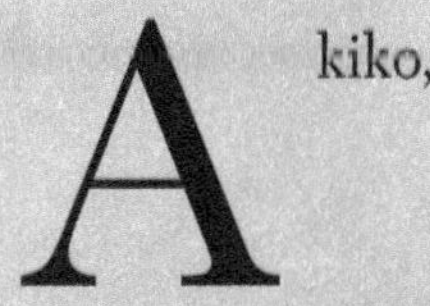kiko,

I was born in Nagasaki in 1862 to a proud samurai name and inheritance. Not long after the Satsuma rebellion, I was set upon by two ronin. I defeated one, but the other escaped. Years later, my home was invaded by three men. I believe one of those men to be the ronin who evaded me. My wife was killed and I was gravely injured. She had been pregnant with our first child. My katana and wakizashi were stolen, along with everything of value in my home. Everything was taken from me, even the honor of a good death. I vowed that night not to rest until my swords were recovered, and I had ended the ronin's lives who had ended mine. When I met you, I was convinced you were a sign from the gods that I should continue to pursue justice for my beloved dead and for myself. Vengeance is powerful enough to make a man forget who he is and what life is for.

When you return home, you will find the key under the sill of the basement window and you'll need to visit the lawyer to sign for my property. Everything we have there is all I have left, and it is yours. I have left his information for you. Blessings.

Daichi

Chapter Twenty-Eight

"Are you sure you don't want to come with me?" Aimi asked, turning to face me once we'd reached the train station.

I smiled and shook my head. "Thank you. I have to go back to Canada." I paused, recognizing the powerful urge that was compelling me to return home, to my friends, even if it might be to say goodbye. "I have family there that I need to see. Are you sure you don't want to come with *me*?"

Aimi laughed. "I have a bit of a mess to sort out here now that Toshi is gone." She clasped my hands with hers. "But you have his mobile number, which is now mine, and my current address so you call me if you need anything. When I figure out what I'm doing from here, I'll contact you."

"Let's not lose track of one another again, okay?" I pulled her into a hug.

"I wish I could travel the Æther, like you," Aimi said into my hair. "It would be a lot easier to see each other whenever we wish."

"Yeah, but isn't it amazing how transportation has changed since we were girls?"

Aimi laughed. "You can say that again. Our parents would never believe what the world looks like now."

We said goodbye, but without tears. Time stretched out before us, seemingly endless. We would be together again soon. Even if soon was ten years from now. I got on the train at Furano and got off in Tottori.

I felt conspicuous carrying two samurai swords through the street, wrapped in Daichi's white robe. I definitely got my share of curious glances.

Yuudai looked visibly relieved when he let me into his apartment. He waited for me to put down my burden and then pulled me into a hug.

"Tell me what happened," he said, guiding me to one of the chairs near the balcony.

The events at the cliffside poured out of me: Daichi's seppuku, how my tamashī was freed, only to be snatched by Raiden. Yuudai's eyes grew round, but he didn't interrupt me. When I told him Toshi and Aimi were there, his jaw dropped.

Tears began to spill down my cheeks as I explained that I had always thought Aimi had betrayed me, but instead she had sacrificed her own tamashī so that Toshi could stay alive and honor his vow to protect me. Once the tears started, they didn't stop, and even when I was finished with the story, I couldn't stop weeping.

Yuudai held me as I wept for Toshi, for the lost years, for Daichi, for misjudging my sister for so long. When I began to sniff and hiccup, Yuudai handed me a tissue and said, "You know what makes me feel better when I'm sad?"

I looked up at him through bleary eyes. "Flying?"

He smiled and nodded. "Want to?"

I nodded and sniffed. "Yes, I do."

We phased into ospreys and took to the air, climbing up high over Tottori. My Hanta vision returned and those same pillars of spinning light were everywhere in my vision. They were wispy and varying levels of brightness, but the sheer quantity of them made my brain stutter. As we soared over the city, I observed that each column of light was coming out the top of every human head below us, and reaching up high into the sky.

Inside each column were two thin strands, spiraling around each other in a rotating double-helix. One strand was pure white, and the other was a dark gray. While some threads spiraled around one another in a clockwise direction, others spun counter clockwise. The ones spinning to the right were bright, lighter columns, some of them so bright that the dark thread was difficult to see. The double-helixes that were rotating to the left appeared darker, smokier, and the gray threads were heavier, dimming the light of the white strands.

Yuudai and I flew out over the sand dunes and the columns of light dwindled to almost none, as there were so few humans, just a few camps and vehicles dotted the sand. Out over the ocean, there were no columns save for the ones threading upward from fishing boats and ferries. We dipped and climbed and surfed pockets of air wafting up from the ocean, and savored the freshness of the ocean breezes.

When we'd had our fill, we turned back to Tottori and made our way home. The white columns grew thick again as we winged our way over the busy urban center. We flew through the columns of light and in places they were so thick there was nothing but swirling threads of white and gray all around us. Returning to Yuudai's apartment, we entered through the open window and I hopped to the bathroom where I'd stashed my clothes.

"What did you think?" Yuudai asked as I came walking out of his bathroom, tugging my shirt down and raking my fingers through my hair. He'd changed in the bedroom and was standing at the open window leaning an elbow on the sill. "Pretty cool, right?"

"Amazing," I said. "Are those their spirits?" I joined him at the window and we looked out over the city.

"Their connection to the Æther."

"The white thread is good, and the gray is evil?"

"Yes, in a very simplified way. I prefer to think of the white thread as love, and the gray one as fear." We crossed the park and made our way toward downtown Tottori. The heat of the day had just passed, and the dinner hour was drawing near.

"And the spinning..."

Yuudai let me think it through.

"When they spin clockwise, it's the love strand that is thick and strong, and dominates the connection. When they spin counterclockwise, the gray thread is thicker and it makes the whole column darker. Am I right?"

"Very clever," he said.

"So, this is Hanta vision," I marveled.

"You would be able to see a possession from how the dark strand changes the column, it looks totally different." The mouth-watering smell of fried vegetables and rice drifted up to us and on the air and made both of us groan. Yuudai looked down at me. "Dinner?

I grinned. "Absolutely."

Epilogue

I descended into the back yard of the house under the cover of darkness and phased back into human. The key was exactly where Daichi had said it would be, under the windowsill of the basement window next to the steps leading up to our back door. I didn't bother to untie the silk robe and put it on. There was no one about at this time of night and I would be inside in a moment.

Bare feet on grass, and pale skin reflecting the moonlight, I unlocked the door with steady fingers. Letting myself into the empty house, I was taken off guard by a stab of loneliness. Daichi and I had been together for so long, and even though all I wanted was to be free of him, it was going to take some time adjusting to life without him.

I walked through to the front door and picked up the pile of mail sitting just under the mail slot. I smiled to see the package pickup notice from the local post office. My backpack, the sword, and my passport had arrived.

I took a hot shower, put on my pajama shorts and tank top, and crawled into bed. I slipped into a deep sleep and didn't wake until late the next morning. It took me several minutes to remember that Daichi would not be here, he'd never be in my life ever again. Birds singing outside my window roused me and as I padded into the empty kitchen, sun slanted into the windows and threw squares of light onto the floor.

I luxuriated in the moment of deciding what to do first for myself. Should I make breakfast at home, or treat myself? One peek in the fridge answered my question, because there was nothing but a couple of rotting limes and a take-out box that smelled like rotting fish. I chucked the bad food into the garbage and went back to my room to dress. Grabbing some cash from under the telephone in the foyer, I pulled on a pair of sneakers and left the house.

As I walked to the post office, I felt the opening of gaping questions in my mind. What did I do now? Did I stay in Saltford and make a life here? Did I want to sell the house and go back to Japan, or perhaps take up the Hanta life and dedicate myself to hunting? Make up for all the lost years when I was no help whatsoever to mankind?

I thought of Yuudai and his invitation to hunt with him. My stomach did a little flip of excitement at the idea of it.

I took the steps into the small post office of our community and went inside. Exchanging the notice for my package, I made my way back home so I could charge my phone. Leaving my phone plugged in and dumping my backpack on my bed, I grabbed the copy of *Brave New World* left unfinished on my bedside table and left the house again.

On my way to Flagg's Cafe, I had to close my eyes and breathe out the gratitude that was steadily building inside me. The day was warm and full of the sounds of life. I was not beholden or responsible to anyone in this moment, and while I knew that would change, and I welcomed it, the moment I was living in right here, right now was no one's but mine.

I knew then and there that I had to tell Saxony, Georjayna, and Targa the truth about my identity. The girls didn't know what they had meant to me in the few short years that I had known them. They were as much my family as Aimi was, and the thought of continuing on with the lies Daichi had spun around us made my stomach sour.

Flagg's Cafe was bustling with people and smelled of eggs and bacon. I ordered a breakfast sandwich and a coffee and found myself a small table outside under an umbrella.

I felt like the richest woman in the world.

"Thank you so much," I said with so much genuine authenticity that the red-headed boy who delivered my food blinked at me.

"You're welcome," he said. "Nice day for brunch outside. Enjoy."

"I will, thank you again." I ate my salty breakfast slowly, savoring every bite. When the meal was finished, I pulled my frothy coffee close and opened my book. It was pure heaven. I allowed time to slip away without marking it.

I read the texts that I had missed while I'd been so focused on my mission. As I was reading, a text from Georjayna popped up.

Georjayna: *I'm back! Just got in last night. I'm dragging my ass today. How are you guys? I have so much to tell you! Like. Seriously.*

I chewed my lip and thought that as much as I wanted to see them, to talk to them, and hear about their summer vacations, I needed a few more days to myself. I wanted to think through what was next for me, and if I was really honest, I just wanted to luxuriate in my new-found freedom a little longer.

I texted back: *I'll be back on Friday. Are you all around next weekend? Sorry I've been so MIA. It's been...* I blinked, searching for the right words. There was no way I could even find an adjective to describe my summer adequately. *Uh... where do I start...*

Saxony: *I'm here! Me too. Nuttiest. Summer. Ever. Targa? You around?*

Targa: *I'm around. Can't wait to see you guys. I missed your faces. Summer was mind-blowing. Still can't believe everything that's happened. I def have news.*

Saxony: *Sleep over? Georjie, your place?*

Georjayna: *Yup, come on over. Saturday afternoon, anytime. Just shoot me a text. I'll get stuff for a wiener roast. Bring your bathing suits.*

Me: *Sounds good.*

Targa: *I'll be there.*

I shut off my phone. So there it was. In a matter of a week, we would all be together, and I would spill my entire story to my best friends. They weren't going to know what hit them.

Born of Air

Book Blurb

She is not what you are expecting. She's not what *they* are expecting, either.

All Petra Kara wants in life is to study Archaeology at the University of Cambridge. And she's close, so close. She's got the grades, she's got the ambition. All she needs now is an outrageous sum of money and experience on an Old World archaeological excavation. *If only she could find a way to get rid of her annoying low-grade telepathy.* There's nothing Petra hates more than a cheat and a liar and it's too easy to cheat when you can read people's minds.

When Petra spies an ad for a volunteer position on an excavation to North Africa, she knows its meant for her. But there is more waiting for her in Libya than broken pottery and human remains. When Petra finds herself in an ancient cave-system with strange stones embedded in the walls, her life changes forever. As her powers manifest, there are those who think they have reason to destroy her.

Petra knows she is far more than just gales of wind. Just how old is she? And has she lived before? But the biggest question of all is: will she survive long enough to learn who she is and what she's really capable of?

Born of Air is the origin story of a supernatural unlike any you've seen before.

> "Such a great book! I had to read it from start to finish!" -Amazon Reviewer ★★★★★

> "Action, intrigue, mystery... and a look into a greater conspiracy..." -Amazon Reviewer ★★★★★

> "They just keep getting better!" -Selena Eckert, Amazon Reviewer ★★★★★

Born of Air is the fifth book in *The Elemental Origins Series* (which can be read in any order) a saga which follows four best friends over one magical summer. If you like incredible abilities, strong female characters, and a little romance, then you'll love A.L. Knorr's YA fantasy adventure series.

Dear Reader,

Thank you for choosing to spend some of your reading time with my stories, without you, I wouldn't be able to pursue my dream career. If you enjoyed *Born of Æther*, please consider leaving a review on Amazon. Kindle will prompt you and give you a link at the end of the book. I can't even tell you how much reviews help indie authors like me.

If *Born of Æther* is the first novel you've read from the now complete *Elemental Origins Series* (which can be read out of order) and you enjoyed it, then I highly recommend you snag *Born of Water* to learn what Targa got up to in Poland while Akiko was busy fighting demons in Japan. *Born of Fire* documents Saxony's adventure in Italy, and *Born of Earth* follows Georjie to Ireland. *Born of Air* is set in Libya, and the final epic ensemble novel will bring all the girls back to Saltford, full circle! If you can't get enough of these characters then you'll be happy to know that the universe has expanded to include 34 titles as of April 2023 and is continuing to grow.

Join my VIP reader list at www.alknorrbooks.com to get automatically updated on new releases, for freebies from me, and notifications whenever there is a promotion. You can unsubscribe at any time and your email will be kept 100% private.

Don't hesitate to write to me, I love hearing from readers!

Love,

Abby (A.L. Knorr)

Asia Minor, 2023

Books by A.L. Knorr

Elemental Origins Series

Born of Water (Targa)

Born of Fire (Saxony)

Born of Earth (Georjayna)

Born of Æther (akiko)

Born of Air (petra)

The Elementals (The ensemble story)

The Elemental Origins Boxed Set (the Completed Series)

Mermaid's Return (Mira's story)

Returning

FALLING

Surfacing

Mermaid's Return, the complete box set

The Siren's Curse (Targa)

Salt & Stone

Salt & the Sovereign

Salt & the Sisters

Earth Magic Rises (Georjie)

Bones of the Witch

Ashes of the Wise

Heart of the Fae

Arcturus Academy (Saxony)

Firecracker

Fire Trap

Fire Games

Legends of Fire

Source Fire

The Scented Court

A Blossom At midnight

A memory of nightshade

A Daughter of Winter

A Prince of Autumn

The Rings of the Inconquo (Ibby's story)

Born of Metal

Metal Guardian

Metal Angel

Elemental Novellas

Heat, A Fire Novella

The Kacy Chronicles

Descendant

Ascendant

Combatant

Transcendent

Visit www.alknorrbooks.com to sign up for A.L. Knorr's newsletter. Get notifications for new releases and free stories.

About the Author

A.L. Knorr is a Canadian, but also a citizen of the world as she travels to exotic locations with her laptop in search of inspiration and authenticity for her stories. A love of yoga, mountain biking, nautical history, and flannel sheets, you'll be as likely to find her sipping a cappuccino in an Italian cafe as you would be to bump into her on a mountain top in British Columbia. At least you know you can always find her online...and she'll be delighted to connect with you. A.L. is married to a Turkish chef (which is brilliant because she struggles with toast) and lives on the Mediterranean coast.

To contact:

www.alknorrbooks.com

www.ingramcontent.com/pod-product-compliance
Lightning Source LLC
Chambersburg PA
CBHW020337310726
48979CB00015B/2403/J
* 9 7 8 1 9 8 9 3 3 8 6 1 2 *